# The Girl Who Laughed At Birds

Leon Rivers

Copyright © 2023 Leon Rivers

All rights reserved.

ISBN: 9798862376456
Imprint: Independently published

# DEDICATION

I never thought this day would come. It means the world to me. To anyone reading this, thank you. If one person reads this book and enjoys it, then it will be worth it.

Of course I wouldn't have been able to do this without my partner in crime, Queenie. I owe you the world.

# CONTENTS

| | | |
|---|---|---|
| | Acknowledgments | i |
| | Prologue | 1 |
| 1 | Life | Pg 6 |
| 2 | The Aftermath | Pg 9 |
| 3 | It Begins | Pg 13 |
| 4 | A Morning Stroll | Pg 20 |
| 5 | Meet The Company | Pg 21 |
| 6 | Not Ideal | Pg 25 |
| 7 | Innocence | Pg 32 |
| 8 | Problems | Pg 37 |
| 9 | Questions | Pg 43 |
| 10 | Decisions | Pg 47 |
| 11 | Hell | Pg 57 |
| 12 | The Job | Pg 67 |
| 13 | Revelations | Pg 71 |
| 14 | Assurances | Pg 80 |
| 15 | Reparations | Pg 85 |
| 16 | Night Time Adventures | Pg 90 |
| 17 | Meetings | Pg 94 |
| 18 | Intrusion | Pg 99 |
| 19 | Trouble | Pg 104 |

| | |
|---|---|
| 20 Two Options | Pg 106 |
| 21 The Bough Breaks | Pg 109 |
| 22 The Hangover | Pg 114 |
| 23 Rendezvous | Pg 122 |
| 24 Realisation | Pg 130 |
| 25 Decisions | Pg 135 |
| 26 Confrontation | Pg 141 |
| 27 Mistakes | Pg 144 |
| 28 Problems | Pg 147 |
| 29 Consequences | Pg 151 |
| 30 Honesty | Pg 156 |
| 31 Waiting Time | Pg 160 |
| 32 Retribution | Pg 162 |

# ACKNOWLEDGMENTS

To all my ARC readers, thank you.
And Shell shell, your ridiculously never ending positivity has helped get this through!

# PROLOGUE

It was bloody cold. That was the only thing that Nat knew for sure. That, and the fact that her keys were nowhere to be seen. Oh, and it was late. Cold, no keys, and it was dark. You planned this well, she thought as she hopped from one foot to the other, her breath adding its own mist to the foggy night time air. It wasn't the first time and normally she would use her back up plan; jumping the fence at the back and through the back door. Earlier, in case of burglars she had decided to lock the back door and now was shivering outside the front. Looking at the empty street around her, she decided she hated the countryside, it was dark and creepy. Apparently, people that live in the Country, or at least not in a city, don't lock their doors. She had tried it on the first night, and did not sleep. She was constantly listening for any sounds that meant someone was in the house. And there were a lot of them; birds, foxes, squirrels, scratching in the night. She had never heard foxes before, and that was forever imprinted in her brain. this, she had decided to have a few glasses of wine in town before facing the screaming foxes. Just without keys.

Nat had not met her neighbours, she could not see a light on in any of the houses in the street. Turning up and banging on the door for.. what? Can I sleep on your couch mister? It would not be a nice introduction, and she might have to see them again. The awkwardness of being that neighbour, was not something she wanted. She had phoned her landlord, which was the only sensible option. Only the absolute neanderthal had not replied. She thought about sending him a message saying the flat was on fire but decided against it. It was day two of her tenancy and she probably needed to keep him on her good side. Her frosty breath did very little to warm her hands as she rubbed them together.

An hour went by, still with no reply from the landlord. Stupid man. She tried to think of different things to keep her occupied. Her job, her bloody parents, she had even tried counting to a thousand. When she got to 400, she realised she was losing it. Her phone only had 5% and she couldn't waste the battery scrolling through so she had given up on that but didn't know what to do next; it was unnerving to be outside. All the sounds that had scared her the night before, well they were much closer now. Her eyes kept on flitting to the side, trying to see in the darkness. She still had not seen any neighbours, or any signs of life really. They probably didn't even live there. "Bloody holiday lets", she muttered. Constantly looking out in to the darkness was not good for her and it was impossible to not give in to the impulse to look behind her. Her neck was aching from the strain, but it just felt wrong out there. She really wanted to be inside.

Nat pulled herself to her feet. On an impulse she walked down the hill, past the dainty dilapidated local church, avoiding the super creepy graveyard, down the crumbling steps onto the waterfront. They looked like they might give way at any point. It didn't help that she could barely see her hand outstretched through the mist. She had a mental image of someone rushing up behind her and pushing her. It was not a comforting thought, she quickened her pace and almost ran to the beach.

The pebble beach ran for miles in either direction, though she could still only see a few feet in front of her. After a little while, she finally found the spot she wanted on the beach, right up to the shoreline. She misjudged it a little, and her shoes got wet. Laughing, she shuffled backwards to get out of the spray. It seemed to be coming closer just to spite her. The night edged by ever so slowly, in a peculiar mix of tranquillity, melancholy and random bouts of panic as she heard noises. It was calmer being on the beach, but she still twisted to look every five minutes or so. The sea had always calmed her. There was something just so… constant about it. There was a time years ago where she would visit it every day. That stopped when she was in London. Now she realised how much she had missed it. It was this unstoppable force, a surge of motion that was… well as inevitable as the tides. And the sound itself, just soothed her.

By now the first rays of light had pierced the sky and with it the birds began to sound off. On a whim she started to imitate them, birds that she had no idea of the name, the odd pigeon that threw its voice to the cacophony of sound and then the gulls that harassed the sea front. And the noise grew, greeting the day to come. Nat's voice rose matching them sound for sound. Getting louder, it seemed to fill the sky and all she could hear were the birds. Suddenly laughing she stopped squawking. She must look so weird; it's the sort of thing you hear people getting psychiatrists visits for, early in the morning screaming bird noises on a beach in the freezing cold, but for a moment all was peaceful.

(***)

He watched her in silence from the pier. She disgusted him. It made him sick to think of her laughing. She had sat, laughed and skimmed stones for hours. Copying the birds as if she had no care in the world. How could someone as horrible as this, be happy? Why was she alive? As if she had not torn away every shred of happiness in his life. She had not even looked back as he walked behind her earlier. He had gotten so close to her he could smell her perfume, the foul stench clogging his senses. She was carefree, and that needed to change. She was poison. This woman, or beast, would feel fear. The despair she had given him, he would return. One day, she would fully know how that felt. She had stood up, and was now walking up the beach.

He followed.

(***)

Nat had given up with the bird calls, she was not even close to their sounds, and she didn't want to get sectioned. She had a day off tomorrow, well today, and was trying to plan what to do. There would be lots of sleeping, maybe a film. It all sounded pretty boring. She needed a boyfriend. Laughing, she thought about it a moment, she would if they weren't all so boring. Her last one had been obsessed with games. Well, the one before last. Who needs a game when they have a girl? That was obviously a short relationship, his looks couldn't excuse him everything. From bird calls, to throwing stones (she never could throw them very far), to considering swimming, she had just about exhausted everything she could think of to do at the beach. Turning on her phone, quickly searching through the messages before it died, she breathed a sigh of relief. Her landlord had finally seen the messages and was at the property. Thank God for that she thought, throwing the last stone into the sea.

It was lighter now, but still fairly creepy. The mist hadn't let up and her nose was starting to drip. As soon as she got in, she was hiding in her duvet for the rest of the day. The gulls were already out searching for scraps, and lights began appearing in the cafes and restaurants for the early morning trade. Her footsteps crunched on the pebbles as she struggled to make her way back up the beach. It felt like her footsteps were echoing into the distance. She stopped to listen, to see how long the sound went on for. The sound however, did not stop. She spun to see a dark figure stumbling towards her. Nat shrieked, stepping back. As he came stepped out of the shadows, Nat saw his face fully. He was a horrifically dirty man, arms outstretched, filthy nails pointed towards her throat. Stumbling to a stop he shouted at Nat.

"You!" he said, eyes wild. Caked in dirt with a scraggly beard, he smelled like a walking bin. "Did I scare you little girl?". Nat backed away, keeping her eyes on him and fumbled for her phone. Her dead phone.
"Who the fuck are you? I warn you, I will scream" She shouted, backing away from him. The man closed the distance again, "Scream all you want, I'm just out for a morning walk. I've got a message for you." He sneered now, edging closer with every guttural word that spewed from his mouth. He snatched at her, pulling her face to face. She felt nauseous being so close to him, feeling his putrid breath warming her face. She tried to wriggle free but couldn't. He had her tight within his grasp, she screamed but those café lights were too far away.
""I know you" he rasped "Who you are and what you are. You can't escape from me. You are scum. You ruin everything. Nat, I know you!"
Screaming she kicked him and ran up the beach. She lost her heels but she didn't care. She ran for a very long time. How the hell did he

know her name?

# CHAPTER 1 – LIFE

Ash remembered the last time he had to get on the train – in costume, make up and tight clothing – it had not gone down well. The old man who he had sat next to huffed and occasionally rolled his eyes over his newspaper. Thankfully, this time no make-up was needed and he could sit on the train quietly, without any glares from the public. Sitting still and quiet however, was a problem. He itched to move, and his lips were constantly moving, reciting his speeches. Ash had rehearsed them daily and knew them off by heart. When auditioning for LAMDA, that is the London Academy of Music & Dramatic art, you needed a monologue. He had picked 'All the world's a stage', partly because he liked it, and partly because it didn't have any tricky words in it, it was either that or 'To be or not to be' and he had seen enough performances of world class actors to not even attempt it. There was no point trying to compete with Andrew Scott, or Benedict Cumberbatch in an audition. Anyway, it paid to pick something traditional and everybody loves a bit of mortality in the morning.

He tried his best to keep quiet, he really did, but the old couple and the guys in office suits further down the carriage would just never understand. Usually, Ash would be listening to headphones and trying hard to not annoy anyone or make eye contact, today it was simply impossible. He hadn't really slept the night before. He had had to rely on an extreme amount of sugar to get him up in the morning. Energy drinks he'd decided, were the way forward in life; that and lots of chocolate. That could have increased the adrenaline but well at least he couldn't ever complain of being too tired. If today went well, he was set for life. He could perform on any stage he wished, star in films. This was his big break and he was ready for it. All his life had been geared to a moment like this. So as 'just sitting quietly' was not an option, he kept up his monologue at the lowest volume he could manage, that and still properly enunciate of course.

The audition was a few hours away and the butterflies had been building slowly for the last few weeks. They were now almost unbearable. To distract himself he begun to stare out at the big tower blocks as the train steamed on. There were millions of people in London, of all nationalities. As the train sped through the countryside into London proper, he could see the immediate harsh mismatch of architectures, and factory development. Well, what he saw was big red brick buildings and thousands of offices spreading as far as he could see. Ash had only been to London as a tourist and it was amazing how grubby the side streets looked. The train tracks always seemed to be behind properties, and he could see the delivery entrances and dilapidated buildings. He didn't remember it being as grubby when he was a kid. It didn't take the shine off though, Ash knew that it wouldn't be like that where he was going. All he had to do was get his foot in the door and he would be free to pursue his life's dream. The train rolled in bringing him out of his revelry and well into the world of London and Charing Cross station.

Ash stopped outside Charing Cross station taking the scene in as the people piled around him, already streaming off out of the gates in their flocks, scrambling to get to work. He had read the sign on one of the tube walls earlier, telling people to slow down. Apparently there had been two thousand injuries on the tube last year because of people rushing. It was so stupid. It was just too much effort to rush anyway. A man swore at him and pushed past, as Ash realised that he was on the wrong side of the escalator. Was it stay left or stay right? He couldn't remember. Once the stream of people passed him, he managed to find some air. His face lit up as he realised he had made it. He was finally where he wanted to be. Striding out into the bustling streets, even the torrential rain couldn't dampen his mood. A dreary grey sky, and tall imposing buildings surrounded him. The gutters were rivers of water drenching any who were unaware of how deep they really went and the wind blew drizzle straight into his face but Ash didn't really see that - as many don't - he marvelled in the city.

He wished he had grown up in London, unparalleled in its wonder; the land of Big Ben, Buckingham Palace, the Thames! The list just went on and on. A world that would soon be his, the whole rank of blacks cabs waiting to take him wherever he wanted to go and the people! Oh he couldn't wait to meet the people of London. The lives they must lead! It was unimaginable. It was so close he could almost touch it. Excited now, almost singing lines from '*As you like it*' he crossed the road. His fifteen minutes of fame was the time it took for the ambulance to arrive.

## CHAPTER 2 - THE AFTERMATH

Ash woke with a start. He had been dreaming again. There was nothing else to do, not with a broken ankle and an inability to get up. His ribs had decided that they didn't like the place they had been positioned before and had decided to relocate. With much assistance from the doctors everything had been rearranged perfectly, so long as he didn't move. According to the medical professionals who visited him daily, the body is a perfectly majestic, sturdy machine, as long as it's not hit by a car. They had taken the wait and see approach after that, telling him that if he just didn't move for a few months he would be alright. Soon he would be out of this place. It was perfectly nice, and much better than he expected. His was the only bed in the room which was downright strange. He remembered waiting for 4 hours when he broke his arm in A and E. He had found out, after some quick questions that he was in fact in a private hospital. Apparently his uncle had him transferred once he was patched up in A and E. He knew it would not have been his parents, they didn't have the money. His uncle Chris, phoned later that day.

"How's it going?" Chris asked with his clipped English accent. Some days he sounded like he could present for the BBC. "About as well as could be expected, I think the driver might have reversed over me a few times."

"That bad? Tricky stuff, crossing the road. Still, one day you'll get there." said Chris.

Ash chuckled, and winced as his ribs punished him for it. "Take it easy on the jokes, it hurts. Thanks for putting me up in hospital. You didn't have to."

"Nonsense, it's no trouble. Anyway, I've spoken to your parents, and they are in a bit of a bind. They… They're working a lot. They can't take the time off to help you." Chris' voice had turned business-like now, as if negotiating a deal or whatever it is accountants do.

"Work is non-stop, and they can't help you while you get yourself sorted. Did you know where there next work trip was going to be?"
"No?"
"A month in Norway, they were meant to be leaving tomorrow"
"Crap."
"Exactly. So we came up with a solution, why not come stay with me?"
"That would be lovely, but how long for? I haven't got my stuff, and sorry but... I want to be back home," Ash frowned as he spoke.
"That's the problem, they won't be home. So it looks like you're with me. It'll be good, I promise. Anyway, look I just thought I would let you know. I have a meeting, bye." And with that he hung up, to a speechless Ash. His parents worked very hard and were always looking for the next big deal. As he grew up they were able to expand the business, and trips like this were becoming more common. The company was looking to expand and create hubs in different markets, they were months away from launching in Scandinavia. Realistically, he knew they had no choice. Still it took him another week before he spoke to either his Uncle or parents.

Ash started to look forward to seeing his uncle, probably because he had not seen anyone apart from the nurse for the last week. Chris had been quite an elusive figure during his childhood, almost immortalized by his absence. He had always been outrageously funny but god as always known for his humour, gave him an unsightly appearance and a job as an accountant. Ash could not think of a more mind-numbingly boring job. He did not know exactly what an accountant did but VAT, spreadsheets and tax forms were some of the dirtiest words in the English language to Ash. It was inconceivable to live a life like that but apparently he earned a decent wage and was happy. And could just fork out money for a private hospital at random. Obviously the job was going better than Ash thought.

It had dawned on him after the first day, he had blown his audition. He wouldn't be getting in to LAMDA. Not this year anyway. It was possible to apply for medical.... Dispensation? He thought that was the right word, however he wouldn't be able to until after the year started. That meant a gap year. He was determined to get in, and if it was not this year, then it would be next year. Going to Chris' would be temporary, until his parents returned and then he would rehearse and act as much as possible. Come to think of it, he didn't actually know where Chris lived. He would have to find out, then work out how to get there. This time hopefully would be more successful.

(***)

The car rolled to a stop and Ash wrestled with his crutches as he prepared to get out of the car. The first glimpses of the town were pretty underwhelming. It was the same as any other coastal town he had seen. A couple of old pubs, a deserted park with the mandatory five or six teenagers huddled together smoking. The standard types of people seem to be in every British town. There was no doubt he would find an old lady that shouts to herself in the street if he bothered to look. The one sight that impressed him was the harbour, they had driven through the town to get to Chris' flat. The harbour was at the bottom of the hill and there were grand archways illuminated in light as they descended. It looked fancy, Ash thought, well a lot fancier than the park

When they arrived at his Uncle's flat, Ash whistled. It looked modern, and it looked expensive. The kind of place that made him feel as if he shouldn't be there. As the luggage was dropped outside, the taxi driver said he would bring up the luggage when Ash had found the right apartment. On the trip, the driver had told him that it had been paid for in advance, with a big tip to make sure that everything went smoothly. After some searching, they found the right number. Ash haltingly clambered up the stairs, hopefully his Uncle would be waiting for him. It was exciting to think that after years of not seeing him, he would be living with him. The last time they met, he had been in his early forties then, balding and skinny as a rake. He was a little man really, as he imagined all accountants were.

Ash knocked. No one answered. Which was a surprise, namely because well... Chris had booked the taxi in the first place. Ash frowned, last time they had spoken, they had agreed a time and said that he would be there. What was he meant to do? He phoned his

uncle, but of course he didn't answer. He was stuck at the top of the stairs, on his crutches. He was not going to be able to rest on them that long, so banged on the door louder this time. This time Ash heard a few gruff curses and a shout of "What is it now?"
"It's me," Ash moved back from the door, as it opened dramatically to reveal his Uncle. It was very close to a full reveal as he was only wearing his boxers. He had put on some weight since they had last met, and looked more haggard. A little bit more worn. "I must have lost track of time, didn't expect you for a little while, come on in." He opened the door as he walked to go and get some trousers. He seemed almost sheepish now but a cry of "What do they want?" in a womanly voice confirmed what he thought.
"It's ok." Ash said "I got the taxi driver to bring up my bag, I will come back later, and I can see you're busy". Chris shouted after him but Ash was off. Shuffling down each step in rapid succession.

He had continued to shuffle down the street and as far as he could go, crutches clicking with every step. The streets all looked the same in a town such as this; even with the streetlights and pubs, it still managed to look rustic and ancient. Meaning everything looked like it was broken, useless or not been updated in the last 100 years. Eventually he found himself by a riverside. He had to stop now, his arms were burning with exertion. It was bloody hard to go far on crutches without stopping. Throwing his crutches down, he fell rather than sat down and laid in the grass, gasping for breath. His Uncle had surprised him. Ash was not expecting nakedness. It shouldn't have been such a surprise. People are people and it was allowed to have women in his apartment. It is what happens in life after all, it *was* shocking though if there was a difference; he didn't know why though. Saying he knew his uncle was human and seeing it were two totally different things.

## CHAPTER 3 - IT BEGINS

He had been sitting and thinking with no real urge to get up for hours now. His arms didn't feel up to it and what was the point? He wasn't even angry with Chris, not really. It had just been a long week, and he really wanted to lie down in something that was not a hospital bed. Instead of waiting for Ash, and having everything ready, Chris was enjoying himself. After a few hours of thinking, he had worked out, it wasn't even that he wasn't the first priority. It was that he was enjoying himself. Ash on the other hand, was miserable. He had been told that his ribs were fine so long as he didn't do anything strenuous, (essentially don't get off the sofa) and that his ankle would take six weeks to heal. In six weeks he would have to go back to the hospital and get the cast removed. From now until then he was going to be immobile, doing nothing and spending every moment thinking about his missed audition. The chance was blown and there was nothing he could do about it.

The riverside was calm, and he had become more reasonable as he listened to the flow of the river. He realised that the path he was on ran close to the main streets. He hadn't paid attention earlier, but it was clear that the streams of people walking past him were either off to do their last minute shopping or travelling back from work. The town must be much bigger than he thought because the flow of people did not seem to be stopping. There was a sense of urgency that they all seemed to have. They all followed the same current, none straying from the path. A giant shoal of humanity, massing in their hordes to do their own seemingly important tasks. Not fish but robots. They all looked as if they had programmed with the same command – *must keep walking*. He even muttered it in a robot voice for a little while to keep himself amused. It was good practice to do accents, one day he may be **Robot#3** in an audition and he was sure he would nail it. A lifetime of copying video game actors and adverts had provided him with a wide range to choose from. He continued to look at the stream of people, trying to see if there was anything interesting to copy about their mannerisms. Most walked without moving their arms, often not fussed that it made them look possessed. There seemed to always be men in suits "briskly" walking. It was a fast pace, usually with one hand in the pocket and one arm swinging up and down. That was a keeper for sure, he had seen it all around England and it was his default merchant banker walk. In both the ordinary and rhyming slang version of the word.

People watching was definitely a hobby of his. He could pick up accents, walks and facial expressions from every walk of life, but also it fascinated him. From his viewpoint he could see a thousand different threads of life, with a thousand different decisions made each day. What were they all having for dinner? Where did they live? What made them laugh? What made them cry? And how did those threads interact? Each person had their own lovers, haters and motivators. It would be amazing to see a life from another perspective. That was one of the things he loved about art, and theatre. From one day to the next he could be different people, from **Robot#3** to Hamlet and back again in a day.

He kept on watching and sometimes his eyes flickered to the extremely attractive in the crowd. It was only in passing of course, but there were a few in the crowd that attracted his eye. One in particular, had captured his attention. It wasn't her figure that he had spotted first, although she was beautiful. She strode through the middle of the street, slowly walking across the path, against the flow of traffic. People moved around her, some tutting or glaring. She didn't even notice them. Puffing on a cigarette and leisurely walking through the traffic, she reached the river and stared out to it. Wearing black heels, a knee length red skirt and a white blouse, she looked straight at him. *Oh shit*, he thought as she started walking towards him.

It had never occurred to him that he was trapped. He thought to run away, but his crutches were out of reach. Ash doubted it was acceptable to crawl away from someone, and it would be more embarrassing than the actual conversation. Putting the thought of escape out of his mind, he laid back trying to appear casual. She had definitely caught him looking, and the clicking of her heels got closer. Desperately, Ash attempted to think of something witty. He still had nothing by the time she sat down next to him. She stared

## The Girl Who Laughed At Birds

out at the river, still casually puffing away at the cigarette. It was a tense time for Ash. He was still at a loss for a decent opener, so ended up staring some more. Not intentionally of course, he was looking past her and deliberately not making eye contact. It helped that she was looking out at the flowing water, As he continued to stare, she finally threw the cigarette away and turned to him.

"So, enjoy what you see?". She had quite a deep husky voice. It was beautiful.

"I...er...was just..." Ash spluttered, he had no idea what to say. Panic flooded him and he felt his face go red. If an asteroid flattened him at that moment, he would have been grateful. Wisely, in his opinion, he closed his mouth and decided to be mute for a while. At Ash's loss of words, she turned back to the riverside and sparked another cigarette. Satisfied he had suffered enough she spoke:

"I haven't seen you around before, who are you?" Ash was grateful for the lifeline, quickly he replied "The name is Ash, you haven't seen me because this is my first day here. What's your name? Do you always come here? I could use some help finding my way around the town."

She gave him a disgusted look and stood up. ""Does it matter? Keep on dreaming boy". And with that she stood up and strode off. Ash sat there, watching her leave. *I really screwed that up, maybe I should ask Chris for tips*."

(***)

Nat had enjoyed that; she needed something to brighten her morning up and he had been such easy prey, a gawking little boy. All boys seem to leer and it annoyed her, why shouldn't she say something? It was like a twenty four hour job for them. Still he had seemed quite broken, she almost felt some sympathy for him but it served him right really. He probably got it for leering.

She had seen him immediately as started walking down the riverside. It was not as if he was hiding it! He was so obvious, that she felt like she had to make a point of it. Some people just didn't know how to be discreet. He could have at least pretended to look at the river or to be doing anything other than what he was doing. He was too young to be unashamed about it, usually it's the old men that were the weird ones. Anyway what sort of name was Ash? It was fun to make him squirm for a little while, but as soon as she spoke to him she knew it was a mistake. He was basic, he was boring and a pervert to boot. She needed somebody fun, and interesting, not a young puppy to follow her around. Nat guessed he was either at school or first year of university. If she did want anybody to talk to, it wouldn't be a person who looked like he still had milk and cookies before bed. Images of him wearing big fluffy pyjamas and a stuffed teddy while trying to work out how to get into a tin of beans popped into her head. She laughed then, ok maybe she had gone a bit too far. He just seemed young and silly. Amusing for a minute but she knew when he spoke that it was pointless. Just another mindless individual, one of a billion people who think they're unique. And interesting. She'd left immediately, but still had another 5 minutes left on her break. She found a bench and sat back against it, watching the stream of people go by. Ash stood up and hobbled down the path going into town. She could see that it took some effort, but he was determined to keep pace with those around him. He was one boring boy, but he did have nice arms though.

(***)

Chris was waiting for him when he knocked on the door.
"You didn't answer your phone". The accountant spoke as he opened the door wide, letting Ash in.
"You didn't earlier; I guess we're even now." Ash shuffled into the room. It was a quaint, neat apartment. Paintings covered the walls and there were huge square windows flooding the room with light. He tried to think whether he knew any of the art, he didn't. They seemed like the sort of thing that was meant to be a masterpiece, but was not immediately obvious to those that weren't experts. The one he was staring at was by a guy called Klimt. Two people kissing, and one of them looked like they were made out of

squares. The woman looked like she had one tiny hand and one massive. Maybe it was worth a lot of money? Ash gave an appreciative nod to the artwork, that seemed like the thing to do. "Ah you're a man of taste I see. Wonderful artist that man is. Knows what to appreciate in life. Any other surprisingly good shows of taste you've got for me?". Ash shrugged as he looked at Chris now, really looked. Chris was a little man, just as Ash remembered but whereas before it seemed as if age had embraced him and matured him, now it looked as if it had broken him. His face was haggard, eyes sunken. The light footed joker he had always been in Ash's mind had been well and truly vanquished.

Instead there was a small man with a scowl on his face.

"Look, I'm sorry about earlier I just wasn't expecting you. You shouldn't have run off like that. I'm doing your mum a favour by having you here."

"I know I'm sorry. Like I said we're even, let's just forget it all." With that exchange Chris gave him a sour look and decided to let things lie. Giving Ash a smile he started giving him a tour, smiling, looking closer to the man Ash knew. It had two bedrooms, a bathroom and a living area with a kitchen attached. It took all of five minutes. All in all, it was a small space not cramped exactly but confined. As they returned to the living room, Ash sat down and the conversation faltered for a while. Chris sat down on the adjoining sofa, staring at Ash obviously about to say something but not quite knowing how to say it.

"Ash... could we perhaps forget about... the way you found me earlier? The company I was with? It is not known around the town and I don't want it to be."

"Yeah, whatever you do is your own business"

Chris looked relieved.

"Good, then food!"

Chris jumped up, animated, bringing back memories to Ash of when he visited the family. When Chris has the energy for it, he would tell tales all night something which his parents often cut short to send Ash to bed, or to put their hands in his ears when something was a bit too adult for his ears. Ash had been looking forward to hearing a few stories uncensored now he was older. Chris warmed to the conversation, and said he had set aside the rest of the day to catch up. So they ordered a vast quantity of Chinese food and Chris decided to pop open a bottle of wine while they waited. Pouring a very large glass of red for Ash, he asked him:

"So tell me, what's going on?" gesturing to Ash's legs.

"Well I got hit by a car."

He snorted "Trust you to pick a fight with a car."

They settled down to wait for the takeaway and found the tension melting away.

"Are you feeling better though?"

"Yes, it's just I feel so useless."

"It'll get better. How is your mother?"

Ash's smile faltered for a second and Chris gave him a smile. They both knew that work came first to the family. When he was younger, they would often take him on work trips. All his friends at school were jealous of the places he got to see, but it was always one hotel after another. They would go out and work and he would play in the lobby and generally get in trouble. Some of the staff would take him under his wing, but they did not like him exploring. Often with the language barrier and not knowing the rules, his parents would come home angry with him for adding to their stress. How was he meant to know you had to pay for the things in the fridge? Or if you watched certain TV it was charged to his parents?

Ash had argued with his parents when he was a teenager and they had decided to get live in support for when they were away building their business. Or as the kids at school teased him: "a nanny". So when the question was asked, what could he say? He saw them about 2 weeks in a month, and they are usually busy prepping for another trip. It was good though, because Chris knew, so they both silently agreed to change topic, finishing their glasses and refilling them, so they both had something to do in the silence.

"How long can I stay here?" Ash asked.

Chris shrugged, spilling some wine as he did so. "Well to be honest, I have a spare room so for as long as you want really."

"I guess I will need a job at some point."

"You might need to start walking again first though."

"Yeah thanks Sherlock." The takeaway had arrived, and been demolished as quickly as possible. They had both ordered too much, and had sunk into their respective armchairs to enjoy their post food coma. Chris grunted looking at his glass and went to get another bottle.

He had obviously been thinking about something for a while. Eventually he asked:

"How do you wash? I mean you can't get your cast wet, do you just not wash?"

"No... we bought this thing, it's basically...It's like a huge watertight condom that you put over your leg so you can get in the bath."

"Brilliant, condoms, why didn't I think of that?" Chris, who had managed to look serious up until this point, burst out in a fit of giggles. They lapsed into a comfortable smile, only broken by occasional bursts of laughter.

"Who is she?" Ash asked.

Chris looked up smiling "you're going to have to be a bit more specific than that."

"You know who I mean, your guest earlier," Ash blushed a bit as he spoke.

"Ah my lady caller, the woman I was having intimate relations with?" he looked at the red faced Ash. "I didn't think you'd be this prudish, yes I had a woman over, it happens. One day it might happen to you."

Chris looked quite content for a moment, then chuckled. "What about you? Any girls on the go?"

"No, I'm not exactly a sex magnet on crutches."

"No I suppose you wouldn't be. Still, in time though." Chris thought for a moment.

"Once you start walking again, I've got a job for you. Running around with me for a bit, doing odd jobs and that."

Ash paused, realising he was slightly drunk, and that he had to be tactful.

"That's a really nice offer, but I don't know how long I would be here. Anyway, I heard there's a theatre here. I need to keep up my acting, to be ready for next year.

"Fair enough, your mum said that you would choose the same thing. I contacted the guy at the theatre, he owes me a favour. How's that for you?"

Ash smiled, and as he went to bed, he realised that coming here might actually work out better for him in the long run.

## CHAPTER 4 - A MORNING STROLL

Over the next few weeks nothing really happened in Ash's world. He had his books, had his computer and spent most of his time wishing it would all just go a little bit faster. The doctors said that it would take a minimum of another month until he would have the cast removed. He was itching to get walking again. It had never occurred to him how useless he would be without a functioning ankle, it was laughable really. The monotony was killing him. He could only read for so many hours until his eyes hurt. Slowly, painfully, he started venturing outside. It wasn't that Ash was weak, far from it, but his arms weren't used to this sort of punishment. Ash explored the town and its old cobbled streets for hours at a time but usually just ended up back at the riverside. It was a picturesque little place, where he felt calm just lying in the grass. Well as calm as he could, being bored senseless, and on a daily basis being outpaced by old aged pensioners. It was the pitying looks that people gave him, the doors being held open for him that infuriated him the most. There wasn't that much wrong with him but suddenly it seemed he belonged to the vulnerable section of society albeit temporarily, and it sucked. At the same time, he did have trouble getting through doors. When he thought about it, he would be pretty annoyed if nobody opened them for him at all. So either way, no matter the circumstance, it left Ash in a foul mood.

It wasn't all bad, he could people watch with a valid excuse now. Some people even came over and talked to him, it was always the old people. It was nice being approached and meeting new people but there was always a tipping point in the conversation where they would get boring or they would start repeating things they said earlier. The worst ones were the people who he met every time, who told him the same stories. To him, nothing was as unbearably dull as a repeated conversation with people he couldn't run away from. With this becoming apparent after the third day, Ash had stayed in for a while but now he felt the need for the flowing river, the calmness of it all.

It was noon, Ash had hours of lying in the grass, watching the water flow by. He had his music beside him but he didn't want it right now. Lying down in the grass, eyes closed, listening to the water trickling by was just blissful. On days like this, it felt the world truly stopped for a while. And it did for him as a voice spoke:

"Hello Ash."

He jumped, and swearing, rolled away from the sound, being followed by laughter from the voice. It was the woman, the one from before, smoking another cigarette. He was amazed he hadn't noticed. She still stood over him, smirking.

"I thought I would watch you this time, seemed fair," she said. "See anything you like?" Asked Ash in a deadpan voice, his heartrate having not returned to normal yet.

She put her disgusted look on again, "No, if you were a horse you'd be put down."

"Oh thanks, I see your still working out how to talk to humans. I can give you tips if you like, maybe don't compare them to animals, and try to avoid murder."

"Well if the shoe fits, though if they saw you I don't think they would bother wasting a bullet."

"Wow... remind me to contact the RSPCA."

She smiled for a second then, then realising what she was doing, changed it to a sour face instead. Dragging on her cigarette she looked away from him, as if she couldn't bear the sight of him anymore. He studied her, noticing that she had a red top on this time. Ash wondered how many she smoked a day, it must be a lot.

He tried another tack "What are you doing here?" "Smoking, what do you think?"

"Ok, so here you are sitting next to me, and I don't know your name. What should I call you?" he asked.

"Call me whatever you want, I doubt we will ever talk again." "Then why are we talking now?" He asked, frustrated now.

"No idea, I have to do something during my break"

Silence resumed.

Neither of them said anything for a while. Surprisingly, she spoke first. "How did you hurt your leg?"

"I had a fight with a car. The car won."

"What did it do? Look at you funny?"

He didn't reply. It wasn't clear to him what was going on, did she dislike him? If she did then why was she talking to him? It was clear that she was not enjoying his company, so why was she still there? She did not look bothered in the slightest that this was a crushingly awkward conversation. She was just breathing in and out slowly, as if this was a lovely relaxing moment between friends.

"Want a cigarette?" she motioned to her pack as she breathed out a puff.

"Don't smoke."

"Pity, vices should always be shared."

"I didn't read that in the Bible."

"Yeah they took all the good parts out," she said.

There was quiet apart from the slow trickle of the water. Ash didn't really know what to do, he wanted to talk to her but it felt more like a sparring match than a conversation. She was an irritating woman, but no one apart from pensioners and Chris had talked to him in weeks. Plus, well, she was stunning.

"What do you work as?" ventured Ash, hoping to at least not get shouted at.

"I sell my body for money."

He paused "Really? Is there much work here then?"

"You'd be surprised, so what about you?"

"I'm taking a break from work."

She laughed at that and gave him a glare, "That was a terrible pun".

"Yeah but you still laughed."

"Seriously though, what're you doing here?" asked the red haired woman.

"I'm an Olympic sprinter, I thought you knew?"

"Oh you're hilarious. When are you on at the Edinburgh festival?" Her voice dripping with sarcasm.

The conversation had lapsed again, but he was happy, he had managed to get a smile out of her at least. He didn't know why she had shown an interest in him, but it was nice to actually have somebody try and communicate with him who was less than double his age. And well, if she hated him, he couldn't do much wrong could he? There was no point trying to impress her if she had already made up her mind; it was that and the fact that he did not have anything to impress her with. Ash doubted that him being lead role in the school play was going to cut it. He risked a glance up, watching her stare out to the river. It was highly unlikely she did sell her body for money, maybe she worked for one of the companies in town. She turned to look at him and held his gaze for a few moments. "Who is the one staring now?" he asked.

"Still you, old habits die hard. See you around little man." And with that she strutted off, walking against the tide of people, expecting them all to move out of her way. To his surprise they all seemed to. *Damnit, that did not go well.*

(***)

She had to admit he was not as boring as watching paint dry. Maybe a small step above ripping her own fingernails out. It turned out he had a sense of humour, and wasn't as much of an absolute wet blanket as she thought. It was a fun way to waste her lunch break. She wondered whether he had come here deliberately to find her but no, it couldn't be. She hadn't seen him since that first day. Nat noticed that he looked trimmer than before, she supposed that was all the walking around on crutches. Obviously he was a grumpy guy and grumpy with her, which made her smile. What right did he have to be annoyed? He was fair game, she owed him this much for staring last time. He should know better really. Still, the amusement had lasted for 5 minutes. He had gone back to being a miserable boy, and she needed to get back to work. She shook her head then, he was a teenager, barely out of school. He was almost a child and she should not be wasting her lunch on him, especially if he was that grumpy.

## CHAPTER 5 – MEET THE COMPANY

Gradually, things started to look up for Ash, after another month of boredom and tedious conversations the doctors had decided to take off his cast. Though happy at the decision they didn't fully prepare him for the moment when the doctor took out what looked like an axle grinder to his leg. His heart took a full week to return to its resting rate.
In this month Ash only had Chris, the accountant for company, all of his friends had run off to university and they only seemed to talk every other week or so. Chris mainly came home tired from work and the general conversations of numbers and more numbers didn't really thrill him. The mysterious woman didn't turn up again and wasn't mentioned at all in that month. Ash was curious but the one time he mentioned it, Chris scowled and did not talk to him for the rest of the night.
So after the month of chasing his tail, Ash was ready to do anything possible to get out of the house, when Chris mentioned again about the job selling tickets at the theatre he grabbed at the chance.

Ash wondered how much he would have to know for the interview. Chris chided him for not having a suit, and they picked the least tatty of his clothes he had brought with him. He limped to the theatre. The doctors had told him to walk as much as possible but he had not managed to go further than a mile or so. After a day of revising potential questions, he made his way down to the theatre which was on the west cliff of the town. He had to go up a mighty steep hill and arrived out of breath at the venue. He paused outside to try and reduce his breathing, heart rate and to at least make sure he was not sweating. There were old townhouses four

stories high, weathered by being close to the sea, a rather archaic dainty church across the road and a hotel where it seemed they hosted drinks before shows at the theatre. Chris had decided to come with him, to introduce Ash to the boss and for moral support, but he said he didn't need the exercise, so had driven.
As they walked through the doors a rather portly, balding, tall man greeted them.
"Ahh Chris, how are you doing? This must be Ash!" He had the booming sort of voice Ash assumed all people of his size had. Ash nodded and said hello, as did Chris. The portly chap identified himself as Thomas Hedley, but Ash was more inclined to call him the fat conductor, it had a better ring to it. He immediately stopped himself, not out of any kindness, but he knew he might actually say it out loud.
"Well when would you like to start?" Asked the conductor (aka Thomas).
"I.... errrrrr," Ash spluttered, "I thought you would want to interview me? I have never really done a job like this, how do you know I will be any good?"
The man laughed and clapped him on the back, "Nonsense boy, you're related to Chris, I'm sure you must be a genius. It's fairly easy, you sell drink, snacks and whatever tickets they want. Ask the age of the person if you aren't sure and count up the money at the end of the night. It is child's play I promise". Sheer panic enveloped Ash but he had no other answer apart from a rather timid, "Sure".

As it turned out he didn't need to worry about working in the theatre, there was always another member of staff and usually they were not that busy so the nights were spent telling tall stories and chatting mindless drivel until they had to close up. It also enabled Ash to meet a lot of the people in the town. As it turns out, the theatre had quite a regular crowd both young and old. There was a lot of interest from the customers as to who the new boy was. Ash had to repeat many times that he was staying with his uncle Chris and that his parents worked a lot so he had decided to recuperate at Chris'. In the next few weeks Ash met all of his neighbours in Chris' apartment block, and the blocks surrounding it. There was a spinsterly old woman named Mabel, who could barely mutter the words "ticket please", so much so that Ash asked for the other guy working with him to translate. Some people were regulars and he did not realise that there would be such a following in the town. The theatre was a multipurpose space, which let local projects rehearse throughout the day. It also showed old viewings of films and new films recorded at the globe by the Royal Shakespeare Company. There were a group of guys in their twenties who always came to see any Shakespeare production, they all seemed to be the same height, same build, all wearing glasses and identical tweed jackets. He didn't bother trying to catch their names, it seemed futile. One day a work colleague of Chris' came in. He made a joke that Chris was rather underhand sometimes. He didn't really know what that meant so he did the standard British thing by nodding sympathetically.

Out of all the staff there, a 21 year old by the name of Steven was his main source of company. Whenever they were working together, Ash knew it would be a good night. He didn't know how well it was reciprocated but Ash definitely looked forward to it each week. Sometimes he would even do extra shifts just for the company. They were quite a duo, and spent a large chunk of their time pretending to impersonate some of the customers. Steven could do Mabel's voice and mannerisms so perfect Ash actually thought she was there sometimes. The highlight of the past few weeks had been when a gas cylinder for the bar pump had gone off. All Ash heard was an almighty bang, the drinks room filling with smoke and he ran out shouting, "Gas!". He had pulled the fire alarm as well. Ash, shaking had explained the situation to Steven who laughed, walked into the room and turned the cylinder off. He had not lived that one down yet. It was explained to him afterwards that they were $CO_2$ cylinders which work just like a tap. Steven kept him reminded of the incident by shouting gas whenever he walked into a room.

After that incident, they had become good friends. They talked about anything and everything, Steven it seemed had started working at the theatre and was now assistant manager. Not that it really made a difference he said, as him and Ash were essentially doing an identical job. Ash later found out the difference was 75p an hour. Steven explained that when he got enough money he was going to move out of "this hellhole" and go somewhere. It didn't sound like much of a plan but, well Ash couldn't blame him.

One day, Ash had turned up for work, expectant as usual to do a 6 hour shift with Steven, however as he walked in the lights were off and Steven was pulling down the shutters to close up.
"What happened? No work today?" Ash asked.
"No, they double booked at another theatre so there is no show tonight. I have a better idea though. Want to go out for a drink?"
Ash felt a rush of excitement as he fully understood what Steven said.
"You sure you want me to come out? I don't know anyone."
"Shut up! If you're weird about it, you can stay here. If not come on, grab your coat."


Ash didn't actually know where the nightlife was; he hadn't bothered looking mainly because he didn't think there was much of one. When he asked Steven, he replied by saying, "You just need to know the right places".
Out they went, locking up the theatre behind them. They walked past the hotel, and went down a steep set of steps winding down toward the seafront. They then walked for about 20 minutes down the promenade. The faint sound of club music could be heard. Ash hadn't really expected to hear anywhere in this town playing loud club music. As they rounded the bend he could see the building where it was emanating from, with bright fluorescent lights acting as a beacon to any who wanted to actually have some fun. Ash thought it was one of the coolest things he had ever seen. As they approached, he saw the cloud of smoke from the groups outside and sound of screams and shouts of everybody inside. He had

never seen anything like it. People were shouting "Hey it's Steven" and running up to greet him. He could feel the music pounding out, and tried to hear what people were saying over the noise.

There were too many names to recall as he was introduced to the lot and Ash tried to seem as if he wasn't bothered. Steven introduced him to Jake, who was vaping and had a bright yellow jacket on and star shaped sunglasses. Jake took it upon himself to take Ash by the shoulders and introduce him face to face with everyone in the immediate area. Ash stuttered through the introductions and felt his face grow red as he was introduced to a group of girls in their early twenties who had obviously had some pre-drinks before coming to the club. He was swept into the club with the crowd and the group pressed him into drinking a shot. As he spluttered on whatever the drink was, they laughed and moved off onto the dance floor, leaving him with a giggling Steven. The music was deafening and he shouted to get the barman's attention.

"I thought you could drink?" Steven shouted through his giggles. Ash grimaced and put the shot on the bar.
"I can, just not whatever that crap is. Want a beer?"
"That was a jagerbomb. Have you never had one before? Wow, this is going to be fun."
Ash ordered two beers and Steven shouted for another round of shots to get him warmed up. They stood at the bar watching as the music changed to 90s dance hits. Apparently, there was a theme every night. This one was "old skool", which seemed to mean everybody dressed as if they were in the Spice Girls or wore double denim. Whatever the theme was, the general message was wear as little clothes as possible and get as many drinks in as possible. Ash had never been clubbing before, and didn't really know what to do. Steven didn't really want to dance, so they made their way over to a booth. They chatted but Ash kept on getting

distracted by the dancefloor. Nobody seemed to care what they looked like as they danced, and he averted his eyes as a girl jumped up on someone and wrapped her legs around him as she kissed him. He returned to sipping his beer.

"So, is this what you were expecting?" Steven asked, who had been watching him blush at the crowd.
"I wasn't expecting anything! But this is insane! Is it always as packed as this?"
Steven chuckled at this, "Ash, this is a quiet night. You wait til you see a bank holiday."

Ash looked around in wonder, and at the same time hesitation. He had no idea what to do. Dancing was out of the question for him. Should he just drink more? Steven hadn't talked for a minute or so and Ash felt it definitely was not alright to be in silence. He tried think of a topic and nothing came to mind. So he ordered two more beers.
After a few minutes of watching the crowd grind, Ash saw a few people stumble and the shouting could be heard above the music. Two guys were shouting at a red haired woman. He choked for a second, realising it was *that* red haired woman.
"Hey Steven, see that?" he pointed at the commotion, "What's going on?"
" Don't know, don't care. That red haired girl is a cold bitch, hardly talks to anyone. She probably started the argument herself," he returned back to his beer.
"Shouldn't we like… help?
Steven laughed, "Nah, like I said leave her to it. Drink up, I'm going to see the rest of the guys," and with that he walked off across the dance floor. In the meantime, the situation had escalated. Both the blokes were shouting and pointing at her. The bigger guy of the two shouted and then slapped her hard in the face. She fell to the floor and stood up holding her hand to her cheek. Ash felt a surge of panic but remained rooted to his seat. She calmly turned around and picked up something, then spun hard and hit the guy in the face with it. The smash could be heard across

the room and the dancefloor emptied as glass went flying. The big guy dropped to the floor and she put the remainder of the glass against the others neck. Ash couldn't hear what was being said but imagined it was fairly forceful. He couldn't believe the bouncer hadn't come in yet. The whole dance floor had evacuated, everybody at the sidelines staring; wondering what was going to happen next. After the red head was satisfied she got the desired effect, she walked out, without a glance or a worry about any repercussions. Ash finally removed himself from the stool and stalked her out into the fresh air.

## CHAPTER 6 – NOT IDEAL

"So just another day of pleasantness for you."
Ash had caught up to her outside and thought it was safer to talk out of arms reach, than surprise her. She spun eyes livid at the sound and focused on him. Seeing who it was, she relaxed marginally and then sighed, turning away and walking on.
" I'm surprised you're allowed out past curfew. Did you get a good stare in this time?" She did not look back as she spoke, her shoes echoing as she walked down the promenade.
"I tried but you were moving too much, all that screaming and glass going everywhere it was hard to get a clear view." He paused his mime as she spun to face him.
"Why are all men such pigs? Nobody helped me in there. And you!" She raised a finger, "You just sat and watched, like you always watch. You're disgusting. Can't you do anything else?"
"Well," he paused, "You seemed quite able to handle it on your own."
"Yeah, well I shouldn't have to should I? I should be able to dance without getting groped."
"Isn't it pretty normal for people to touch each other when they dance?" He asked.
She gave him a withering look and walked off.

(***)

Men were disgusting. She couldn't go anywhere without them leering, harassing her or evidently following her. What gave them the right? Honestly, she thought, what use were they? Tonight was her night to get away from it all, to have a moment in peace and enjoy herself. It had been a long time since she had had a stress free night. Always there was something to worry about or someone to look after. She had moved out here to get away from all the stress and actually be free. No one would know her here, or have awkward questions or be any hassle. And yet immediately, some feral fuckwit with an ego, decided that he was hers. *Eugh, why did they have to be such idiots?* She hadn't planned on hitting anyone that night. Her only plan was to sit and get drunk on the sidelines watching the young adults make tits out of themselves. It was a good sport and she enjoyed it. Today of all days, she joined in with the dancing, just to see whether it was as fun as they were making out. It was good, but as the song finished, the trance had vanished and she realised how bad the smell was. Sweaty youths closing in around her, like herding cattle. She stalked off the dancefloor, finished her drink and walked to the toilet on her way out. On her way back, the two louts had grabbed her. They were laughing to themselves and seemed surprised when she didn't appreciate their free hands. They had seemed even more surprised when she grabbed the bottle. She smiled then, that had been the only thing that had gone right that night. The timing couldn't have been better. *I hope he is digging glass out of his face for weeks. He deserves it.*

On and on she thought about the parasites that had disturbed her night. She was so engrossed that it came as a surprise to her that she was out of breath. In anger, she had been walking a lot faster up the hill than was advisable. She checked herself, and slowed down a little. As she crested the hill, she regained her breath and turned into the alley shortcut to her home. She just needed to get home now, maybe spend the night looking for flats in other towns. Maybe she could join a convent, at least then she could go about her day in peace.

She didn't see the swinging arm that knocked her off her feet. She did spot the kick that hit her hard in the stomach but was unable to do anything other than watch it impact. Retching and coughing she attempted to get back on her feet, spluttering she made it to her knees, eyes streaming. Her assailant grabbed her hair, ripping her head back to look her in the eyes.

"Remember me?" He spat at her. Nat could see the blood still dripping from round his face. He looked mad with anger. "You won't be able to forget me soon. I will haunt your fucking dreams. You asked for this." His voice shook with rage, his hands holding her hair harder until they were almost coming out of the roots. Pain shook her. He pushed her head roughly to the floor, Nat wriggled and almost managed to get free. He grabbed her, ripping her clothes as he forced her back to the ground. She cried out as he pushed her head to the ground once again.

"You hurt me today, I think it's only fair I do the same." He spoke in ragged breaths as he slowly pulled out a glass bottle, making sure to keep it in Nat's eyeline. She squirmed and screamed as he laughed. "I take it you understand how badly you fucked up today." He let out a shout of rage as he swung the bottle towards her face, his face twisted in a snarl of anger. Neither of them saw the Nat's knight in shining armour come out of the dark and swing, or as Nat calls him, the Leering Boy.

(***)

Ash had finally decided in one of his worst thought out decisions to follow the red head. She had already stalked off into the night but after asking in the club, he was told that she lived on the "west side" or somewhere near there. He didn't know much about the town, but they were already on the "west side". It didn't seem as if any of the locals knew the difference between east or west. It was clear that there was no point following her, as he would not find her and she would no doubt shout hysterically at him when she came to the realisation that he had escalated from leering to stalking. Even so, he started out in the direction she had stormed off. She didn't look happy and Ash was sure he should try and recover from what he said. Even if he could see how the guys were getting confused by her signals. She was quite confusing sometimes, and never really made it clear whether people should talk or not. He definitely wouldn't mention that this time though, that would start her arguing again.

Working out what to say to her was harder than he thought. *Sorry you attacked two people with a weapon?* Or *Hi, I've stalked you home without you asking, on the off chance you don't hate me forever.* It did not take a great stretch of his imagination to picture her reply: *You are disgusting, I will phone the police immediately.*

Or more likely: *Sure thing, stay there while I get my chainsaw.* The more he thought about it, the more he realised how bad he could look in this situation. He arrived at the top of the hill and decided to call it quits. He could walk all night and not find her, or worse he could find her and be savagely beaten for being alive.

A scream rang through the night, and he ran towards the sound. He found the redhead on the floor with someone over the top of her, glass bottle in hand. Picking up the first thing he found he swung it as hard as he could at the attacker's head. He dropped like a stone.

Nat looked at him with ice cold eyes, struggling to control her breathing; her shirt ripped open, her head cut from being knocked down and the realisation that she should be in a considerable amount more pain than she actually was. She looked at the body of the floor and tried to raise a foot to kick him. It wasn't possible, oh she wanted to, but her body did not seem to be able to work properly yet. Her hands were shaking from the shock. Panic surged through her, willing her to run, flee, to get anywhere away from here.

Nat shakily got to her feet feeling the grazes on her palms; she refused the hand offered and when realising who it was she shoved him away, "Don't! Just don't come near me!"

Ash backed away, raising his hands, "Fine, no trouble. Are you alright though?"

"Yeah fucking amazing, can't you tell?" her voice dripping with sarcasm. Rubbing her hands through her hair she looked down at the bastard who attacked her. He hadn't moved since Ash had hit him. "Do you know who he is?" Ash asked. The attacked looked a lot better out cold. Dry heaving, he realised he might not be out cold. "Some creep from the bar. Jack or something. Who cares?" As she spoke she kicked his foot just to make sure he was not going to wake up any time soon. She then turned to walk away. "Shouldn't we call the police or something?" Ash asked.

Nat gave him a scathing look, "Jesus, where did you grow up? I'm going home, and locking the bloody door. As for him, you can stay and babysit if you like but I don't think he is going to be very happy when he wakes up."

"Ah, you have a point, at least he didn't see me."
"Oh you're such a hero."

"Can you say anything without sarcasm? If you don't mind I will walk you home."

"What?" screamed Nat, "What makes you think you can come anywhere near me? You think because you help me out one little time that I would forget that you're as much of a creep as he is! You're such a pervert, you're disgusting. Why can't people just leave me alone?". He stepped back as she raised her hands to him. Speaking slowly he said "Because you're hurt and I want you to get back safe? Hence why I came after you, I just wanted to make you're ok? People can be like that you know?"

"How do I know you won't do what he did?" She asked. "Not everyone is scum y'know? Some of us our nice people." "I don't believe you. Anyway what type of creep shit were you trying to pull. Following me? That's not nice people behaviour." She looked him up and down, obviously not trusting his word. "I'm not like that guy. I'm one of the good ones." She looked at him, wondering whether she trusted the weirdo. He ruined it with his eyes flicking down to her ripped shirt.

She erupted at that. She had had enough of the night, and screwing around with another creep was not making her feel any better.

"Go on then, prove it! Go away, leave right now. Get out of my face! I bet you won't. Typical man. You won't do anything without an ulterior motive."

Ash, slightly shocked, slowly backed away and started walking. Nat looked at him walking off, surprised that he actually did what she said. Her eyes had started to well up, it had all been too much today. She needed that red wine and some sleep. She called out to him though as he left, "Hey Ash, my name. It's Nat."

## CHAPTER 7 - INNOCENCE

Ash awoke in a haze, his vision blurred, synapses only half functioning. There was no real reason for his grogginess, he hadn't drunk much. Slowly, as he began to recollect what had occurred the night before, he remembered her name. He couldn't help but smile when he said it out loud: Nat. It suited her. She was infuriating, like a little mosquito. Or a big one, he reflected as his mind reminded him of the image of her with bottle in hand smashing it into the brute's face. Wincing, he replayed the events of the night before. He was still in two minds as to whether to call the police or not, but he wouldn't do that before he spoke to Nat. If it was possible, he wanted to avoid making her any angrier. It was her choice really anyway.

Leaving it as he did last night, he was worried. They hadn't even phoned an ambulance, against all of his better judgement. Nat had persuaded him not to, well more she had told him to get away from her in no uncertain terms and he made his way home. It had taken a long time to sleep, and even then it was only fitful bursts in between images of the man still laying in the alleyway. Ash didn't know whether he'd wake up in five minutes, or not at all. Still he did kind of deserve it. When he finally hauled himself out of bed, he knew that no matter what came out of today it wouldn't be good.

Chris usually brewed a pot of coffee in the morning and today was no exception. Ash came into the kitchen to see him reading the newspaper, his face drawn into a scowl. He didn't look up as Ash walked in. Ash had a little moment of panic as he wondered what Chris knew.

"Everything ok?" asked Ash trying to sound as casual as possible.
"Yeah, just had some bad news at work. Do you have anything planned today?"

Ash breathed a short sigh of relief, but the knot of tension in his gut would not budge, "No, nothing really. I have a day off. Thought I would relax and have a bit of a lazy day." Chris looked at him sharply. It seemed apparent to Chris, that Ash was trying way too hard to be casual, but he let the moment pass without questions.

" You can't be lazy forever. How much are you making at the cinema anyway?"

"About £100 a week".

"God that Thomas is tight. Well if you ever get bored and want some more money let me know. I have a few errands if you get interested."

"You serious?" Ash was broke. Chris had been giving him money on a weekly basis, but it was embarrassing to rely on him for everything. His parents had sent him some money, but it hadn't been enough to do anything really. There were games he wanted to buy, and he definitely couldn't afford the train fare to go into London. Not only that, he needed better cameras and lighting for his videos.

After a long time considering what to do next, his plans had not really changed much. He was going to LAMDA and this time he was going to get in. If anything, this year could be a blessing. No local groups had any openings for actors, not apart from the local amateur dramatic society. He had spent a few weeks rehearsing there, and couldn't keep a straight face as a softly spoken man in his sixties wandering around the stage trying to play Heathcliff. Ash still wasn't sure whether he had actually read the script or not. It had been so painful that he simply never went back.

The opportunity of LAMDA was there for the taking, and there had to be a way of giving himself a head start. He had racked his brains for weeks and then stumbled on the solution scrolling through Youtube. There were videos of people doing terrible re-enactments of famous movies, it was almost as bad as the local theatre. The solution was simple, he would film soliloquies and scenes from famous plays and put them online. He would do all sorts of suggestions and often deliberately messed with the original scenes from films or plays. His personal favourites were "puck on helium" and clips of "Notting Hill" or "Love Actually" in the style of Shrek. Maybe it was not the most traditional way, but then if he tried that, they may never let him in. So whenever he said to Chris he was having a "lazy day", they both knew that he would be alone in his bedroom often having two way conversations with himself. It was accepted now, but there were a few strange conversations in the first couple of weeks. Chris finished his coffee and started getting his things together to go to work. Starting up his laptop, he went in search of the next project.

(\*\*\*)

It was often commented Detective chief Inspector Frank Heath was not a happy man, but today he had reason to be. Some days he appreciated the early morning; waking up to the birdsong, morning coffee, relaxing with his first cigarette of the day was bliss. In those moments he would be contented and quite often the day would quickly travel downhill from there. This morning, he had rushed all but the cigarette as he was rudely awaken to an emergency call in the early hours of the morning. At 3am, a victim of the name Jack Lasson, address 34 Waterloo Crescent, was found comatose at Madeira walk. Immediately, he had taken action by closing off the area to the local public, assigning a constable to protect any evidence and contacted the forensics department that suspected attempted murder had occurred. His next unenviable task was to contact his boss who would then be in charge of the investigation. The Chief Super, hallowed be his name, had all the major crimes in the Kent area, so when contacted, gruffly told Frank not to screw around and get it sorted. Chief Superintendent Bishop would be in charge, but in reality that meant Heath would be running the show. More specifically, he told him in no uncertain terms to not fuck it up and remember his ABC's. ABC's in this case being - Assume nothing, Believe nothing, and Check everything.

He assessed the area and decided there was not going to be any further contamination. Further in this case meaning: whatever sewage it was already mired in wouldn't get any worse. He dreaded to think what the results were going to show up. Setting out the rendezvous point, he then stopped to take his bearings on what had happened. He was interrupted in his musings by a constable muttering about spending valuable police resources on what could simply be a medical problem. Heath gruffly pointed out the dent in

Lasson's head that was reported by the ambulance crew and told him to shut up. That stopped any questions for a short while.

The questions did not take long to restart though, as once the constables had got their heads around the fact it was foul play, they then asked the question: "Who did it?" Which unfortunately was a very good question. The first step in any major investigation is to interview, so by 6am, he sent out any uniformed officers to start canvassing the area. Many didn't answer the door, and the ones that did weren't too helpful. Most were shocked that there were police officers at their door, and of course there were the usual curtain twitchers. He reminded each officer that they had to have an interview record of each witness who would talk to them, they often forgot. After a while, Frank joined in with the door to doors, to speed up the case. He had hoped Lasson would wake up, and identify his attacker making the case open and shut, but the messages from the hospital were clear that they did not think that would happen anytime soon. In fact it seemed that they weren't hopeful of his chances. He was medically comatose. Already they had started looking at the CCTV in the area, trying to get a sense of what may have been covered. It being a tiny little town, there were not many cameras at all in the area. Not even a ring doorbell to be seen. Some of the witnesses had heard shouting at 10pm the previous night and some boy racers were hanging around at 1am, and he made a record of those that mentioned this. None of the houses were close enough to have a direct view of the alleyway. Some thought it was foxes, some said it was a whole gang of youths. It was often the case with witnesses, they seemed to want to say anything to catch your interest.

On his last call, he had been to two homeowners, who were both in their 50s, and both still in their dressing gowns. They had chatted amiably with the constable, he had brought with him, PC Phelps and they had been wrapping up the interview when a man in his early twenties came down the stairs. He ran down the stairs, gasping and asked:

"It was Jax wasn't it?" Frank frowned. They had not disclosed the name of the individual to anyone, as they were still attempting to contact his next of kin. Immediately, he started writing the conversation down.

"Jax? Who's Jax?"

"Jack Lasson, he got in a row last night. Ran off, and didn't text back. Hasn't answered the phone since."

"What can you tell me about last night?"

(***)

Nat hesitated, the man she was talking to towered over her. The sceptical look on his face was not weakened in the slightest by her smile. He was over six feet tall and broad with a slight belly, the protective jacket he had on didn't flatter him; he was a policeman. A DCI, whatever that meant.

"I asked you Natalie, at what time did you get home last night?" he repeated. He had tried to get her to invite him in, but she had ignored the hint.

There was no way he was coming in, "Is there anything wrong officer?" she tried her best smile. Most idiots fall for that. Looking at his face, it seemed he was not one of them.

"I understand there was an argument last night and reports of a fight in the club. Do you have any knowledge of that?"

"I was groped last night but I didn't feel the need to call the police. Did somebody put in a complaint then?" Nat replied as innocently as she could manage.

"No, there was another matter we were called to. For the third time, when did you get home last night?" His expression did not change, but his voice took on a sterner tone.

"Oh no, what was the other matter? You don't seem too upset I was assaulted last night."

"On the contrary, I am very concerned for everyone's safety, we are just making enquiries at this stage."

"I was home early, after that happened, I walked straight home with Ash. He stayed over. You can check with him. He will back me up of course."

"And how can I contact this Ash?" he said notebook ready.

Nat panicked. "He... err... has lost his phone and I can't

remember where he lives."

"So this man that stayed round last night, am I correct in saying you don't have his number or address? Is he real? How do you talk to him, carrier pigeon?" The policeman said drolly.

" He works at the local theatre, we meet up for drinks afterwards." "Ok, I'm going to talk to 'Ash' and it would probably be best if you don't leave town for a few days."

As soon as he left, Nat's legs buckled. As he had started talking to her the lies just flowed, perhaps she should have told the truth, but the police were always looking to lock people up. It was never prevention with them, just to punish the victims after the event has happened. They weren't there for her when she got attacked, were they? No, she had to fend for herself. Speaking of which, she needed to find Ash. No doubt the *leering boy* would confess all in seconds without her there to help him.

## CHAPTER 8 – PROBLEMS

Chris was putting his jacket on when there was a knock at the door. It started as a knock and then progressively became a hammering until Ash clambered to answer it. Looking at Chris, it was clear he was not expecting visitors and they both stared as the door opened to reveal Nat.
"We need to talk," she said, striding into the room. She looked serious, he could tell because she wasn't smoking. Glancing up and down at Chris, she gave him a filthy look. Chris, for his part, chuckled and looked at Ash. It was a look either meaning *do you mind telling me what this is?* or more to the point *who is this nutcase?*.
"You don't write, you don't call. Yet now you want to talk?... Nat," Ash said. He said her name with some relish, the opportunity too good to miss being the first time he could use it. "This is my uncle Chris, Chris this is Nat, who is a friend I met in town." Glaring at them both, she carried on her pacing, muttering to herself. Both Chris and Ash were waiting expectant, as to why she was in such a hurry. After a minute of looking Chris up and down, she whispered, "It's ok. Another time." And walked out.

As the door slammed, Chris asked, "What was all that about then Ash?"
"Not a clue. See you later right?"
"Yeah, I'm working until 4 o'clock, I only have one client's accounts to sort out. You know reconciliation and all that."
"Erm, no I really don't, bye," and with that Ash ran out of the room, taking the steps down two at a time. He caught up with Nat just as she was walking down the stairs. Lightly, he touched her arm to get her attention.
"What was all that about?" he asked. She twisted as he touched her and kicked him hard between the legs. Well, she tried to. The stairwell was too confined and she hit his thigh instead. It still hurt as Ash fell to the floor wincing.

She hissed, "I told you! Don't touch me!" and continued walking down to street level. Ash, after regaining his breath, followed slowly, making sure there wasn't an ambush waiting for him. Turning the corner, he found her sitting on a brick wall waiting for him.
"I swear to god woman, you are actually insane! That really hurt."
"Well maybe you will learn your lesson next time." She rummaged in her pocket, sparking up another cigarette. Not looking at him, she spoke, "Want to get a drink?".

"Are you joking?" Ash spluttered, "I want to know what the hell is going on. You storm into my house, storm out even quicker, kick me in the balls and then offer to go for a drink at 9 in the morning? Are you on a serious amount of drugs?"

"Ok, coffee then?" She called over her shoulder, flitting off down the street. Ash followed, shaking his head. It wasn't like he had anywhere better to be.

The coffee house was a chain that offered coffee and muffins at crazy high prices, but did at least have comfy chairs. He sank into one of the armchairs, relaxing back when Nat decided to calmly destroy his morning: "I had a lovely morning, I did my washing, had a beautiful shower and then a policeman asked me about the man you nearly killed and put in a coma last night," she said whilst preening her nails, legs idly crossed.

"What? You waited all this time to say that?" he had spat his coffee across the table and had been shouting. He glanced round and lowered his voice after a few glares.

"What did you say? Did he believe you about him attacking you in the alley? Why didn't he ask me?" She had stopped preening her nails, and was dabbing her face where the coffee had sprayed her.
"I told him no such thing, I informed him that we had spent the night together, getting rather drunk and then you left in the morning."
"Why in the world would you say that? If they ask I'm going to tell them exactly what happened. Everything!"

Taking a breath, she looked him in the eyes and leaned in, "No you're not, and I tell you why not: firstly, because I have told them a different story, and that would make one of us liars and make us look guilty; secondly I wouldn't back you up and then you would admit to putting a man in a coma for no reason. Plus they wouldn't believe you anyway. I had a fight with him in the club and you as a jealous or overzealous boyfriend could easily be motivated to hurt a man over that. So you, are going to say exactly as I said: that we spent the night together and you left in the morning". He didn't know how long his mouth had been open, and closed it, so he looked less like a goldfish. She couldn't be serious? Of course they had to go to the police. They had committed a crime, and the police would find out for sure. He had checked her face, to see if this was just a prank, another way for her to get back at him but no, she was not joking. It dawned on him that if he did admit it, well… she was right. It would be confessing for no reason. He didn't want to lie, but he damn sure didn't want to go to prison.

Hesitantly, he checked that nobody was listening to their conversation, then turned to her.

"Why would you even do this? I helped you out, I saved you. You don't blackmail or bully someone who saves your ass. It's not what people do."

"Well it is today," she smiled, "I'm not going to prison for attempted murder because you're useless at life. If we had handed ourselves in straight away, they would have locked us up and kept the key. You know that, and that's why you didn't do it. The police, they just want a scapegoat, and what is that scumbag worth to you? Why would you give yourself up for him?" she finished in a flurry. A thought occurred to him.

"Anyway since when have I been an overzealous boyfriend? If you hadn't noticed I only found out your name last night." She snorted, "Don't get any ideas, you're too whiny, too skinny and too much of a pervert for me anyway."

"Wow, you really know how to make a man feel happy. Right I'm going."

"You can't go, we need to talk about this."

"There is nothing to talk about. I'm not lying." He had thought about it, he would just explain what happened. They would understand. The police would know that he did nothing wrong.

Ash stood up, leaving his coffee on the table. He felt light headed but pushed through it. How could she be this brutal? He had never met such an infuriating, and evidently immoral woman. It was like she didn't have a moral compass, or if she did it wasn't pointing the right way. Despite what he had said to Nat, he wasn't sure what to do. Lying wasn't a good idea, but he didn't want to go to prison. Truth be told, he cared a lot more about betraying Nat even if she was psychotic. Probably more so because she was psychotic. Should he lie? Should he just leave town? That would look pretty suspicious. He thought Chris might give good advice, but could he ask him? If Ash had done anything wrong, well then telling Chris would make him part of it. That simply wasn't fair, so was not an option. He walked out, leaving Nat behind, out of the café into the arms of a six foot tall balding policeman.

## CHAPTER 9 - QUESTIONS

The tall balding man with the thick eyebrows stepped in very closely and spoke "Are you Ash?"
"Yeah that's me," stuttered Ash. Glancing around, there was no way to conveniently slip past the policeman. In his imagination, he had an image of him running of down the street, sneaking away, evading the law and the policeman comically looking around wondering where he went. Reality hit hard as he looked at the man's stern face. Not only was there no chance of escaping but what would be the point? Running away? He might as well take a taxi straight to prison. Bringing his gaze back to the policeman, he realised that he actually could get past the man. It looked like he had deliberately left him a route just to see what he would do.
"How can I help you officer?" He said in the lightest tone possible.
"Some people would think you a very guilty man Ash."
"And why would that be?" Ash kept his voice even and looked the policemen in the eye. It was difficult, and he had trouble knowing how long to look at him, that and where to look. The problem was, he knew he was in trouble. It was impossible not to squirm under the man's gaze.
"Well I talked to the lovely Natalie this morning, your very close friend, although she doesn't know where you live, or your phone number. I gave her my contact details and said I would like to talk to you rather urgently over the nasty business of a young man in a coma. I then find out that she found you first, proving she was either very confused or lying. Then you didn't call me. Some people would think that you're a very guilty pair and that you were solidifying your alibi."
*Ah Shit* thought Ash. Nat had set the ball in motion by lying, there was no other alternative really. The only question was, what to say? He set out in trying to clear up the mess, hopefully without his voice cracking. Attempting casual he opened his mouth:

"Well hearing that a man who sexually harassed you has ended up in a coma is quite distressing, I thought she made me stutter and stumble but that takes it to a whole new level." He swallowed, "Last night was amazingly stressful for her, and I imagine seeing you in the morning was just as scary. She came here to try and calm down out of the house, and I often have coffee here. She told me you wanted to see me, but your card was still at her house. I thought of calling 999 but I didn't want people to think it was an emergency. Where is the local police station for the record? It will help me out if I'm ever in trouble."

He tried not to be smug, he really did but that was the smoothest reply he could ever have hoped for. Tying up all the loose ends and explain how they had met up today was a stroke of genius. He was still shaking and the very real thought occurred to him that he could go to prison for this but if that happened then he was going to lie through his teeth until the end. He didn't think he would like prison, Nat probably even less. The smugness obviously showed as the policeman's stern face became sterner, "I will do better than that, I will show you. If you will come with me please Sir. I think Natalie might enjoy the trip too, come to think of it."

Fighting back the bile in his throat, he stepped into the backseat of the police car. The policeman went back into the café, but Nat was nowhere to be seen.

He had never been in the back of a police car before but then again he had never lied to a police officer before. It was a day of firsts, and now he was on his debut trip to the police station. The policeman, DCI Heath apparently, had not handcuffed or manhandled him in any way. Heath described it as a little trip to the station, to show him where it was and to talk about the events of the last day to "assist with inquiries". No arrest yet, which gave him some relief but it dawned on him after some time that he couldn't be in a worse situation. He was on his way to the place where they usually put people in jail. And they knew he had lied, and was involved in some way with a man being hospitalised. He began to hyperventilate in the car as he considered that his morning outing might have been his last day of freedom. Realising that the police officer was watching his every move, and his panic, added more fuel to the fire. By the time they had reached the police station he was drenched in sweat. They put him in an interview room, closed the door and left. He'd assumed that they would want to talk to him straight away but after half an hour or so they had still not returned.

Sitting in the room alone, he had time to plan, to organise in his head what he was going to say and come up with the best response. He did that for around five minutes, unfortunately his brain kept on throwing images of him in prison or rotting in a jail cell until the end of time. Did they still have steel bars in prison? This next conversation could be his only chance to avoid jail. Yes, there were quite a few reasons to panic and his fantastical mind thought up every one of them, each worse than the last. He had heard the smaller boys in prison didn't get treated very well at all. He almost started doing press-ups there and then to prepare for prison. He had let his mind run away with him and after an hour or so he slowly reigned it in. Laying out the facts, he was in trouble, and he knew this but the first thing he needed to do was calm down and get through this interview. But how? And then he smiled. Simple really, he would act.

(***)

DCI Heath and Police Constable Phelps had watched him stewing for the last hour. He had muttered to himself but nothing intelligible. It was obvious to anyone that he was panicking and in over his head. Phelps hadn't understood why Heath was in such a good mood until he saw the suspect. Heath knew he had to work fast to identify what happened and who the perpetrators were. This "Ashley Merson" was an amateur. He had never been in trouble, had no dealings with the police and was obviously dreading the encounter. It looked like things were starting to look up. After two hours of letting him panic they decided it was time to start the interview.

Heath reintroduced himself and his colleague and notified Ashley that he was being recorded so as to not have any misunderstandings later down the line.

Ash's face paled as Heath read out the caution: "You do not have to say anything. But, it may harm your defence if you don't mention now, something which you later rely on in Court. And anything you do say may be given in evidence. I must also tell you that you are entitled to have a lawyer present at this point and that you are currently free to go, but while you are here you might as well answer a few questions."

Heath paused to see what the reaction would be. Although the suspect's face was pale and very sweaty, he met his eye and said, "I don't know any lawyers, plus I haven't done anything wrong. So I think that answers the question. I have somewhere to be this evening, so this won't take long will it?"

Ash had thought long and hard about this. He knew he could get a free lawyer, everyone knew that but would a guilty man turn down a lawyer? It would throw them. He just needed to put doubt in their minds. There must be something good from looking like a baby faced teenager.

Frank raised an eyebrow at his counterpart and then proceeded with the interview, "So that answers my question then, you're not guilty of anything?"

"No," Ash smirked back at him.

"It is often said that everyone is guilty of something. You never stole sweets? Broke into a construction site? Rode a bike pissed?"
"Not me. By that logic, does that mean that you're guilty too?"
There was a natural pause as Frank rethought his conversation. He probably shouldn't have started the conversation on a tangent. If Bishop heard that start to the interview he would not be happy. "Ok, can you tell me about last night then, and when you left Nat last night."

"I didn't, I stayed over. I'm sure if she talked to you, then you would already know that."

"Yeah, sorry, I misspoke, can you go over the events of last night please."

As they were speaking, a knock came at the door. Heath turned angrily to see who had interrupted him. He was beckoned out of the room by a rather nervous constable. Stepping out the room, his face grew darker as he listened to what they had to say.

Hours later, Ash left the station trailing the Asian man in the suit, passing a stream of police officers, he couldn't believe his luck. All day, dreams of him being handcuffed, or taken away in a police van with a hood on had been flashing into his brain. He thought he might never see open air again. The lawyer who had accompanied him out of the interview room had opened the front door to the police station and held it open for him. Ash walked through, his face breaking into a smile. The world was looking up. Once outside the lawyer gently grabbed Ash's arm.

"Today does not change anything if the gentleman wakes up from his coma and identifies you as a suspect. Neither can I stop you from incriminating yourself through your own idiocy. Whether or not you were the perpetrator of a crime, step very carefully Ash. You're on their radar now." The lawyer sifted through his jacket pocket and sourced another card, handing it over to Ash, "This has my number on it, call me if ever the police arrive again. Are we clear?" Ash looked at the man's level gaze then pocketed the card. He had tried to speak earlier but their seemed to be a lump in his throat.

"As I told the police officer, I was with Nat all night." "Yes I'm sure you were, though if one were to speculate it seems like you only just missed the time frame. It's lucky there are no cameras near that part of town. I'm sure if the alibi was shifted by a few minutes a jury could be convinced."

"Well.. I... Er..." Ash had found it a lot easier lying to the policeman than to this man. A thought then occurred to him. "Why did you come to help me anyway? I can't pay you!" The man stopped midstep and turned back towards the police station.

"Well, if my services can't be paid then I could simply get the police to rearrest you."

Dread filled his mind. The man was being serious, he looked left and he looked right but there were policemen everywhere all walking into the station. Anyone running away from a police station was going to be caught in seconds. The lawyer stepped in quickly, grabbing his arm and hauling him off down the road, chuckling to himself.

"Sorry that was my little joke. Call it a wake-up call. You're messing around with the big world now, there are consequences. I owe your uncle Chris a few favours, he has been very good to me. So I promised I would be your lawyer until this blows over. I don't do pro bono work so I guess this could count. Don't ever lie to me and we will get on just fine. If you lie to me I can't protect you." They reached the car, a beautiful white Audi, and got in.

Now he was staring out of the window into the darkness from in leather seats, radio 4 on in the background; he had been wondering earlier how he was going to explain his exact predicament to Chris. He had made plan after plan but the sense of doom had got stronger and stronger until it almost engulfed him like a weight on his chest. Not only did Chris already know, he had sent a lawyer in to go represent him and hoist him out of the fire. Considering Ash's parents would disown him. How the bloody hell did Chris know that he was in trouble?

The Audi turned into Chris' road and they both went upstairs, breath frosty in the night air. They clambered up the stairs and Ash let himself in. Sitting in a cosy armchair was Chris doing his best to be calm and composed, although he did ruin it by jumping out of his chair when Ash walked in. Ash's attention was drawn however by the redhead, who had stopped mid-pace when the door opened. "Thanks Matt, I had every confidence in you. If you ever need a favour phone me up," said Chris grinning broadly.

"I wouldn't dream of it Chris I already owe you enough as it is." As the men shook hands Ash continued to stare at Nat.

"I thought you got out of that habit boy?" She asked looking him up and down, an accusatory look on her face.

"Well, I can't but wonder why you weren't in a police interrogation room side by side with me?"

"Well some of us know the bar staff and where the exits are to a building, we aren't all as naïve and complacent as you are."

"So you saw him and didn't think to warn me?" Ash shouted, "All I have done is help you out and you screw me at every chance you get."

Matt and Chris were smiling at the two of them shouting. "Boys, Girls, best behaviour now. If you have any information pertaining to the unfortunate incident of the young man in a coma, unless it's ever going to come to light again then I suggest you bury it unless you want the neighbourhood to know, you're shouting loud enough as it is. Now, Natalie as you are involved with Ash's case, by default I will be your lawyer if needed to protect Ash's interest, unless you are charged and then I will get another trusted colleague to defend you. Say nothing if the police question you, just phone me. Are we clear?" Matt focused his level gaze upon her. "Crystal," she smiled sardonically. "Right let's get to business, wine I think is needed. Have a good bottle Chris?"

"Of course," and with that Chris raided the wine rack and gathered four glasses. Ash, Chris and Matt all found a chair to lean back into, Nat after a minutes deliberation settled to perch on the end of one. There was an awkward silence, only broken by the pop of a wine cork. To Ash it didn't really feel like a grand occasion. Then again, he thought, he might have only had prison meals for the next twenty years if it were not for these two.

Looking at the sour expression on their faces, Matt and Chris broke out into loud laughter. Once they had wiped the tears away Chris asked, "Ok, so why did they question you Ash? Your lovely friend Natalie hasn't been very amiable company, she threatened to leave a few times too," he gave Matt a wink, "Yet another woman I know who doesn't see sense."

Nat stood up, spilling her wine. Ash quickly jumped in before she tried to assault any more people. "Erm, there was a guy. He's in a coma. Nat had an argument with him in the club and then an hour later," Nat coughed, "After we were at Nat's I might add, he somehow gets injured and happens to be in a coma." Ash looked Chris in the eye, Chris however just looked at the lawyer and chuckled. Leaning back into the sofa, he asked Ash, "And you two are jumping about as if the apocalypse is happening because he attacked Nat in the club then you went home without interacting with him at all? What do you think Matt?"

Matt was smiling into his wine, Chris' voice tinged with amusement. He was definitely enjoying this.

"I think these two are in way over their heads. I'm just trying to think of who did what, it isn't really important though. Not unless new evidence comes up," said Matt tucking into his wine. "Is it young love do you think? Maybe they take people out for kicks, or did he just annoy you guys? Who's next on your hit list?" "I don't have to listen to this shit, fuck you guys." With that she leapt up from her perch and stormed out, slamming the door behind her.

(\*\*\*)

Nat slammed the door on the way out. She should never have helped him. She had only gone to Chris because she couldn't think of anyone else. Ash would have blabbed, useless little boy he was and then they would both be in prison. He wouldn't even last as a day in prison. They didn't know anything, these pretentious pricks. The accountant who thinks he can make a call and sort the world out, the lawyer thinking he can solve everything with a click of his fingers, and then we have the leering boy. A boy who thinks that everyone should like him, thinking that the world owes him something; that if he put his hands out then the world will just jump into his palms. Though today he hadn't leered at all. Nat might have to call him something else but for the life of her she couldn't think of anything else apart from useless. Surely that was worse than being a pervert, he was beyond even that. It was not clear to her whether he was really fucking stupid or... well no, it was clear he was really fucking stupid. What sort of person doesn't realise there is a policeman outside? The car and big flashing lights, they were the giveaway. At first she thought he was being lovely and buying time for her to get away; it turned out he didn't even realise. It would have been misguided but it could be cute to have someone look out for her. Instead, he stood there gormless as the world fell apart around him. She snorted at a thought, *his only use in life would be as an organ donor.*

She could hear gormless calling down the stairs for her. *Well, he could take a long walk off a short pier.* Nat went quicker to avoid the inevitably of another desperately needy conversation. She could imagine it now:

"*Oh Nat, why don't you like me?*"

"*Errr well maybe your face, how you talk and everything about you?*"

"*Oh but can I still follow you around like a lost puppy?*"

It wasn't as if the rest of them were any better really, they could all die in a fire for all she cared. God, she needed a drink. It was definitely a rum day. She felt a hand grab hers, and she swung her other fist towards her assailant. It was Ash, the stupid fucker. He threw himself backwards. Nat, off balance, fell straight on top of him. She stayed on top , hitting him as hard as she could. His hands were protecting his face so she started hitting him lower instead. " I told you! I bloody told you! Don't ever touch me again." She had found a gap through his hands and managed a clean hit on his nose. Nat, breathing heavily paused for a second to catch her breath, Ash grabbed the opportunity to stop the onslaught by holding her wrists.

"You should have told me about the policeman," said Ash, hoping she wouldn't take the opportunity to punch him. As he felt her breath on him, he tried to work out whether she would stoop as low as headbutting him, "Or you shouldn't have lied in the first place but you did. So you are well in my debt so can you stop trying to cave my head in. Isn't one person in the hospital enough?"
"Shut up!" pushing her hand over his mouth, she leant down on him. He stopped talking, but his eyes dropped down to her top. "You're disgusting!" she shouted. She slapped him, and slid away. "That was not my fault, you were practically flashing me." "Well you took your chance didn't you," she said readjusting her top.
"And you may have given me a black eye. Are we even?" She gave him a disgusted look and starting walking down the concrete stairs, "Not even close."

Grunting, he followed at a safe distance.

"Seriously though, we need to work this out. We both want to, so why not have a truce?" Ash asked.

"Because then it means you might think I could stomach your company."

"Wow, after all of our chats and heart to hearts I thought we had become close. Don't you feel the same anymore? Let me guess it's not me, it's you," he stepped back swiftly as she reacted at his tone. She paused to look at him. He backed up a few steps more just in case.

"No it is you, you creep. I mean why did you follow me in the first place? Why did you help? What do you want from me? Or are you just here to stare?"

"People can be nice you know, they aren't all the worst of the worst."

"And aren't I so lucky that my knight in shining armour turned up right when I needed it. That's a glorified term for a stalker by the way."

He blushed but said quietly, "Should I have just left you?"

"Maybe I would have been better off." And with that she walked away.

## CHAPTER 10 – DECISIONS

It was a strange set of days after the incident with the policeman. Ash had been waiting for the world to implode but it hadn't. Night after night, he had gone to sleep wondering if police were going to come and raid the house, dragging him out into the street in his pants. After Matthew and Chris had talked, no more was seen of his lawyer. As he set foot out into the town, it was all, well.. fine. He didn't really trust the calm peace of the town anymore and expected the authorities to be behind every corner but no one magically appeared behind a bush. There was nobody shouting at him, no police riot van to take him away forever. He was a free man. Chris didn't mention it again, and if anything was more cheerful than ever. They had decided not to notify Ash's parents. Chris had said he didn't want to upset them while they were working. He had decided not to go to the bar again though, he didn't think he was ready for another night out like the last one. As for Nat, she wasn't anywhere to be seen. He had her number now but she didn't answer. He had tried every day, sometimes leaving messages but there was no way of not sounding desperate. It did occur to him that he couldn't say anything on the phone in case the police listened. He didn't know whether they actually did that, but it would be a terrible way of getting caught out. When he thought about it, she just seemed ungrateful and very angry at him no matter what. She didn't seem like a nice person, so maybe it was for the best. Now, however, it was time for work.

He opened the door to the theatre with a knot of fear in his stomach. Did anybody know about the other night? Steven was there already, restocking the fridge.

"Hey Steven, what's new?"

Steven stopped what he was doing and rested his hands on the case of Fanta he was stocking.

"Like you being carried away by the police?"

"Yeah, misunderstanding. I think they thought I was somebody else! Scared the hell out of me."

"Yeah well Hedley wants to see you. He is not very happy, seems like he didn't get the memo about it being a misunderstanding," He put on a gruff voice, " Hiring a straight up criminal, this is what I get for hiring people from out of town."

Ash tried laughing it off, "You know me, what does he think I've done?" Steven shrugged at this. "Ok, well if anyone says anything, point out that the police don't usually let the criminals walk around." "Fair point, go see the bossman, but it's not going to be good news. Maybe I will spot you a beer sometime, might have to wear a stab vest though."

Ash made a joke and swore at him, hopefully that would convince Steven that he was not worried. That was way too close to the truth for him, and if everybody was thinking it the police must be too. He had to find Nat as quickly as possible. Taking a second to get himself together, he walked up the steps to the fat man's office. He had thought of just walking off, but Chris had told him to continue as normal.

His office was on the floor above the bar, all wooden and looking like something that was in fashion in the Victorian era. The office itself looked more like it was out of a law firm than part of a theatre and that the man himself should be running around in a white wig. The rotund man was stuffed in his chair, looking at him as if he were going to pull out a gun or piss in the corner. Hedley took a deep breath and spoke with a gentle but firm voice, "Ash, I hired you because Christopher is a wonderful man and he vouched for you. Suddenly you become involved with the police and I simply can't have that my dear boy," he was shaking his head as he spoke. Ash jumped in with, "The police haven't charged me with anything, he obviously thought I was somebody else."

"The police didn't charge you with anything? That's hardly the first thing an innocent man would say is it? That may be the case however it looks damned terrible for the business with the case still unsolved. Take a few weeks off until the case is resolved, I will pay you to the end of the week." Ash didn't argue, there wasn't much point. They had talked for a little bit more but it was made clear that there was no future for him at the theatre. As Ash was leaving, he asked Hedley what the real reason was that he couldn't have the job anymore. "My boy, this is a very small town. People talk. And what they are saying is 'oh look at that boy, the police almost locked him up'. It's simply not good for business."

*This is not good,* he thought. He said goodbye to Steven, getting out of the theatre as quickly as possible. Steven watched him as he went.

Ash walked down the street, not knowing where to go or what to do. He would have to break the news to Chris that he had lost his job. That was secondary to the fact that he had to find Nat. He walked around the riverbank for a few hours, even going to the café that they had been at before. She was nowhere to be seen. He had thought about dropping by the nightclub but he did not want to go anywhere that place ever again. After three hours, he gave up.

As always Nat found him not the other way around. He had been laying in bed trying to think of "get rich quick schemes", although Chris had banned him from investing in Crypto. He had screamed when she walked in without knocking. It was not his proudest moment.

"Jesus woman, don't you knock? You could try and at least not scare me every time you see me."

"Well surely that would spoil the fun."

"Two weeks, it's been two weeks since I've seen you. Now you turn up as if we are fucking besties!"

"There you go with the moaning again Ash, Jesus, you really are a self-pitying prick aren't you?"

"Wow, so did you come all the way here to insult me?"
"No, actually...." Nat hesitated. Ash panicked, she never hesitates. "What?"
"You are coming over to my place."

He stared at her, mouth open.

"How about for a second date we go massacre an old people's home?"

Nat gave him a droll look, "And no, we told the policeman we spent the night together, he's started asking people at the bar about us. You have to play your part. We're going to spend a lot more time together."

She said in a baby voice: "Come along little boy..."

And with that she walked out the room.

(\*\*\*)

Two hours later, Ash was sitting tentatively on the edge of Nat's sofa in her house. It was not his comfort zone. He could not have felt more awkward. Nat had almost dragged him to her apartment, sat him down and then went upstairs without a word. He had stared at the carpet for a while, then the ceiling. There was some music on upstairs, some sort of jazz; he doubted it was 'in the mood' music. It was probably more likely that he would be stabbed than invited into her room. He had been waiting for ages now and it seemed clear that she wasn't coming back down. Ash had questions that needed answering though. If it were so important for them to be seen together, shouldn't they actually know each other a little more?

He rose and started to look through the house: at the pictures on the wall, the clean kitchen – he even had a look in the fridge. There wasn't much there apart from a few beers, some chicken and a half empty bottle of wine. Ash finally noticed what was bugging him. The flat didn't seem lived in. It was hotel clean, but there was no clothes being washed, no mess from the previous meal. He shouted upstairs to get her attention but got no response. Doubtless, she would think him a creep if he went upstairs but why bring him over if she wasn't going to talk to him? Did she want him to go upstairs?

He walked slowly up the stairs, he had decided after all that if she had invited him in then she could at the very least talk to him. He could see pictures on the wall he doubted she had bought them herself. Going up the stairs, he raised his voice, not needing any more accusations from her.

"Hello?" He shouted. No answer came back. "Crazy lady?" Still there was no reply. " I am coming up the stairs, do not attack, I repeat do not attack."

Ash had no idea what she was doing or even which way to go. There were three doors, all looking equally uninviting. What if she was doing something he did not want to see? Maybe she was in the bathroom? He knocked on each door in turn nervously, slightly worried she might spring out with a baseball bat. Nat opened the door from the room closest to the stairs. She had cracked it open marginally, just big enough to see a single eye with her hair dangling down in front of it.

"Yes?"

"Are you going to talk to me?" He asked.

"No, I don't think I am," and with that she closed the bedroom door on him. Well, he hadn't seen a bed but he imagined it was her bedroom. Slinking back downstairs he wondered what to do. Should he leave? He knew it made sense to stick together but well, did it? He had alibied Nat when she had needed it but how did they know what the policeman thought? Them spending more time together could look conspiratorial which the policeman had already pointed out so helpfully. It was all a bit bloody confusing so he turned the TV on and cracked open a beer. If she wasn't going to talk to him, she couldn't complain if he raided the fridge.

"Still here I see," Nat had come down the stairs silently and Ash jumped at the sound.

"Yes for my sins," he said whilst his heart rate climbed back down to normal.

"For our sins," she corrected him. Looking at her standing in the doorway, she sounded relaxed but she didn't come into the room, nor did she sit down on the steps. It looked like she was ready to run if he moved.

"How do you know this will work? Spending time together might make us look more suspicious," he asked not moving from the sofa. "I don't but it's my best guess. After saying we are, then not seeing each other again looks a bit suspect too."

Ash nodded at that, there was no point arguing. Nat had decided. "So, how is this going to work?" he smiled broadly, "Do you send a bat signal into the sky or write "booty call" on the grass with fire?" She glared at him but only for a moment before rolling her eyes. "Before you get any ideas this is not a booty call, you are to all extents and purposes a toddler."

"I'm eighteen!" he shouted, ruining the effect by his voice going higher than he meant it to.

"Like I said, a toddler. Come back after a few breakdowns and then tell me how good life is." Furious, he stood to go.

"Well if you want to just sit there and insult me all day I will go now."

"No, don't do that," Her face softened slightly, "I.. want you to stay. If we have to be here together maybe we should have some ground rules." As if to emphasise her point she went into the living room and sat down. In a single armchair furthest away from Ash. She still looked like she might decide to beat him if he said the wrong word. A thought occurred to him, she was probably more organised than that. So he looked inconspicuously around the room, sincerely hoping there was not a taser lying around.

Ash sat also, determined to meet her eye and to actually get some sense out of her for once. He spoke first: "Rule number one, no hitting me. No insulting me all the time," he said levelly. She glared at him and then did another eye roll.

"It sounds like you have more unreasonable conditions, so get it over with."

"If we are going to do this then let's actually be friendly to each other."

"Fuck off."

Ash smiled, "See my point?" He asked as he stood up to leave. "Ok fine," she held up her hands in defeat, "Oh sit down boy, you know you have nowhere better to be." It was a depressingly accurate description of Ash's life. The few friends he had, had gone to university leaving him stuck in a town where the average age was enough to get an OAP bus pass. He did not in fact have anywhere or anything better to do.

She sighed and looked him, "I won't hit you or insult you unless you deserve it. For the friendly part, we are not going to be best friends but I'm sure we can actually not kill each other." She stopped at a look on his face.

"Oh," she chuckled "Too soon?".

"You think? I could have killed a guy, not the best thing to have on your CV."

"Well if this goes wrong, our lives are gone, however pitiful yours might be."

"See that's what I mean about insulting me," he paused though as a thought struck him, "Did you ever think you would go to prison?" Ash asked.

"The thought has occurred to me," she said as she stretched back and pushed her hair back from her eyes, "I don't think it would be too bad. It depends for how long. Always thought it would be a good time to learn a language or get a degree. I think there is quite a bit of free time."

"Ha. What would your degree be in? Insulting people?"

"I always wanted to do law," she said quietly.

"Do you not think that might be incompatible with $1^{st}$ degree murder?"

"Well no actually, there are famous stories of people going to prison and becoming lawyers. I mean it's not as if they can ruin the profession's reputation is it?"

"No I guess not."

"Speaking of which, what do you know about this lawyer guy? He seems proper creepy."

"I don't know much about him. He has a fancy Audi.

"Wow Sherlock, you are going to do well in life."

"Well what was I supposed to find out. I was a little busy worrying about going to prison for a long time."

"Yeah well you wouldn't survive a week. I bet you would throw even your own mother under the bus to avoid that."

"Not true," his voice raised, "That is not true, I saved your ass didn't I."

"Ah true, therefore proving that everybody at heart is truly selfish."

"How so?"

"Well if you ratted me out, you would be in prison by now making best friends with Ronnie and Reggie."

"Who?"

"Don't worry, some gangster then."

She was right in a way, he thought, if he had wanted to be honest he would have said the truth. Instead he was realising that he had lied to the police, and he would have to lie in court if it ever came to it. That was perjury, another prison sentence on top of accidental maybe murder. Could he do it?

"Ok, I am selfish," he said, "But tell me, what's wrong with the lawyer?"

"Think about it you melon, a random lawyer which even you, with

your infinitesimally small brainpower, realised had a very expensive car. Do you think accountants in a two bed rented flat in this shitty town can call on somebody like that. Not only a lawyer but a specialist defence lawyer who turned up very quickly. That is some shady shit." She had held his eyes from the moment she started speaking and it took him a while to compute what she was saying.
"Yeah, Chris said he was owed a few favours."

"Favours? Favours?" She asked, becoming animated, "What sort of favours do you think he did to get that much pull? I don't want to be anywhere near your uncle or his weirdo friends."
"Well that's not much of a thank you for them getting us out of prison."

She spun towards him, eyes flashing, "You don't get it do you? You weren't even arrested, you could have said no when they asked you. You weren't charged with anything. So our story held true, and we weren't in any danger. We aren't in any danger unless they find some evidence, or the guy wakes up."

"I was handcuffed!"

"Ok they may have arrested you, but they didn't and that might have only been because I ran away. They didn't have any evidence and would have only held you for a day."

"I thought the 'anything against you may be given in evidence was the caution?' Where are you going with this anyway?"

"What do you think that policeman thought, when he brought some young kid in for questioning. Some naïve little toddler who went gooey and almost pissed himself when the police turned up? The policeman was just asking questions, establishing a time frame and shit like that. Then all of a sudden, head honcho from a criminal defence lawyer firm turns up to sweep the investigation away. That's like using a sledgehammer to crack a walnut. The lawyers shouldn't have been able to react that quickly, and they know how highly unlikely it is for a local accountant to get a big business firm in that quick."

"Oh shit, but so what if it is a bit strange?" Asked Ash. The way he saw it, they were less likely to charge him if they knew a big company was protecting him.

"If you were just a naïve little screw up, it would be fine. But now they have found a peculiarity, a boy with some serious protection that looks above his means. It means they are now paying attention to you, and think something shady is going on." That made him pause for thought.

There was a knock at the door. They both jumped and scrambled up to look through the windows. There was a police car outside and the same dour policeman was standing there, straight faced as ever. Nat swore and then walked slowly to the door. Ash half hoped they could just hide upstairs, when he suggested it she had told him he was all manner of stupid and then continued to the door. They had waited for a while, hissing at each other as quietly as possible. Had they been loud enough to hear? Nat had clearly pointed out they could see the lights on, sighed and opened it.

"Hello, Mr policeman. I can't call you that. What is your name?"
"DCI Frank Heath, I did tell you last time."
"And badge number?" She asked. His straight face grew a little darker at that.
"And why would you need that?
"Well I think it is highly inappropriate for you to be contacting me at this time of night. We were having a nice night in and I think this is starting to qualify as harassment. You have my details if you wanted to contact me, I will be happy to put a complaint in."
"Ah so true," he said regaining his composure, "but I have good news for you, the unfortunate victim of a truly barbaric attack has shown some improvement recently. You will be happy to know he will be able to be questioned in the next week or so." He said this with a bright smile on his face, it was not pretty and it suited him like a pig suits a tiara. Nat's face stayed emotionless but even Ash could see if she gripped the door any harder it would come off its hinges.
"While this is wonderful news, I'm not sure why we would care."
"Well it is now possible for you to make a complaint against him for sexual harassment if you so wish."
" I would rather just let him crawl back to whichever hole he came from."
"Is Ash here by chance?"
"Yes, he is."

"Oh good, you can tell him the good news." He gave a very short nod of the head and strode towards the car. As the car drove off and she closed the door, and she slid down the wall. She started crying, helplessly ,"Oh god, how the fuck do we fix this?".

Ash just stared numbly, thinking the exact same thing.

The policeman had got into the car and driven away. He had not driven far, parking up round the corner and sat on a park bench as he waited to see if the two suspects did anything. Ash had a squeaky clean record and was essentially an aspiring actor just starting out in life. He would probably end up working as a barista for the next ten years the man thought grimly, *arts degrees don't get you far*. Nat had a more complicated past, with a few mentions in the police records. She was never charged or implicated in serious crime but it was not normal for a name to pop up that many times without something being wrong. Either she was incredibly unlucky or very good at getting away with things. He had a hunch that something was wrong with their story. A fight at the club and then the guy is in a coma an hour later. Add in the expensive lawyers and something was deeply wrong. He had been working 25 years on the force and had not seen such expensive lawyers for a kid with no real money in the family. As he sat there, munching on his sandwiches packed away in his pockets he waited to see what their reaction would be. If they reacted badly, he would know they were guilty. He did not bother to get a warrant, it would have tipped the lawyers off. So he was going to do sit and wait, and in his own time too. He would know if they decided to run. He did not need to wait long.

## CHAPTER 11 – HELL

The next day Ash woke early at Chris' flat. In truth, he had not slept at all the night before. Not once had he closed his eyes, but he had tormented himself with visions of that horrid guy pointing at him in the court room screaming: "It was him!" Images of line ups where he was pointed out and led away in chains. Coffins closing shut on him, the prison cell doors closing, plunging him into darkness. Dreaming of nights in a prison, in pitch dark with the awful rasp of a cellmate waiting to pounce on him. He shook, he cried, he screamed into his pillow. Ash knew his brain had run away with the possibilities of never ending punishment but he could not stop. The only lessening of the outpouring of emotion was when he simply could not cry any more. He knew the guy had not seen him, he could not possibly name him, but that did not help. He had tried in the very brief moments of sanity to think of a plan. How to stop all of this happening? Nothing he had thought of could solve any problems. It would have been better if he had never woken up, but then Ash would be a killer. He did not think he could cope with that, even in helping someone else. No, if he had killed the man he would have turned himself in. He had better morals than that, he couldn't be a killer and walk the streets. He would have to walk to the police station and hand himself in. His life would be over, his career in tatters. Maybe he could do a prison production. He chuckled grimly, as he imagined a prison production of Les Mis with gruff bearded killers singing I dreamed a dream. He groaned, turned over and put his face back into his pillow.

Ash eventually crawled out of his bed and stumbled to the kitchen. He needed a coffee and he had not eaten since lunch the day before. They had planned to eat at Nat's and the sudden knock at the door had ruined that. After an hour of trying to reason with an inconsolable Nat, he trudged home. It was when she had started shouting and throwing plates at him he had decided it was time to leave. It was 5 o'clock in the morning and everywhere was dark. He stumbled around for a while and gave up, turning the light on in the kitchen. The light burned his eyes but it was irrelevant, he did not really care. Monotonously eating toast, he sat in the low light of the living room, illuminated from the kitchen, staring at a patch on the wall. He finished the toast, and just kept on staring. These might be the last few days of freedom he might have. Should he run? Should he hide? He had gone through fear, anxiety and panic only a recurring cycle through the night. Now even that was gone, he simply did not have any more fear left. Or more to the point, his brain simply did not register it. It was waiting for later, when it could pounce once he could function.

An hour later, Chris stepped into the kitchen in his dressing gown. He glanced at Ash, and made himself a cup of coffee. "Want anything?" He asked as he pottered in the kitchen. Ash merely shook his head. Chris stirred the coffee and then threw the spoon in the sink, which rattled loudly in the quiet room. He strode from the kitchen to the living room and sat on a chair opposite Ash. "I don't usually like to point out awkward situations, truly I prefer to ignore them. But it is hard not to point out the obvious," he spoke slowly looking at Ash's red raw eyes and messed up hair. "Which is?"
"You don't seem like you're ok." Ash snorted derisively at this but did not say anything. "You go out with this girl, well woman, and come back like a shrieking banshee. What happened?" Ash still did not answer.

"Is she secretly a vampire?" He gave an encouraging smile to the pale faced Ash. It was a weak joke, meant to calm him, which was clearly not going to work.
"Ok," Chris said, changing tack, his voice growing sharper, "You can sit here and wallow in whatever shit you've got going on, but the way I see it is that you only have two options. Sort your shit out, or sit there moping until you die from bad hygiene practices." Ash jerked up at the sound of his voice. He had never really heard him raise his voice before, or be angry with anyone. "So I am not going to put up with self-pity and being a miserable sod around the house. If you won't tell me what's wrong, then I

don't care but don't spend all night crying and then tell me you're fine. You're meant to be a grown ass adult now."
"Yeah well this shit is serious," Ash finally said, "It's going to ruin everything. I'm absolutely screwed."

Chris looked at him, eyes worried, "What is it?"
"The guy in the coma. He is getting better. He is going to be interviewed next week."

Chris quickly put his hands up, "I don't want to know remember. I am not involved. So you are sitting here whining because this guy could cause problems? Well that's just bloody stupid. Are you going to do anything about it?"

"What do you mean?"
"Like phone your bloody lawyer to get ahead of this?"

He had not thought of this. It would seem like a glaringly obvious mistake to make, but he had just been thinking about his sudden demise and whether he would see the sun again in the next thirty years. "He's not my lawyer though is he? He seems quite expensive?" Ash asked this hesitantly. He was fully aware how lucky he was to have had the help however, Nat's comments had stuck in his brain. Something was odd there and he did not know what.

"Like I said, he owes me from a while back. He will sort it all out, and if it costs more money I will pay him," Chris said reassuringly. Ash looked at his uncle, feeling a surge of gratitude for the man. Someone was going to help him; he knew though, that it would not be enough.

"Maybe we shouldn't bother him. It's not going to be worth the money, they are going to arrest me anyway.

"Like I said, sort it out or sit here until the world falls on top of you."

"I guess, you're making sense, I know, but I don't see a way out." He didn't feel much better, but at least he could breathe which was a improvement on the night before.

"Right," Chris clapped his hands together and stood up, "get showered and changed, then come with me."

"Why? Where are we going?"

"You have nothing to do, you have no money, your sitting here moping around wasting away. I think it's time I start getting my money back on you, you're going to come and work for me."

He did as he was told. . He showered and changed, scrubbing at his puffy eyes in the mirror. It was an improvement but not by much. A polo shirt, jeans and trainers were all he could find and as he came out to see if Chris was ready his uncle barked a laugh. "Ha, no chance, where do you think you're going? The skate park? Go find a shirt." Ash had only packed a few items and did not have any shirts so borrowed a shirt and trousers from Chris. The jacket did not fit and they weren't the same size in shoes so he had to settle for the darkest trainers he could find. He walked back to the living room and saw that Chris was dressed and ready to go in a sharp looking grey suit. It really did make him look professional and confident. It was another side to his uncle that he had not really seen before: The powerful businessman. The suit was in fact very similar to the one Matt was wearing when he had come to pick Ash up. When he asked him, Chris joked that either they both have great taste in clothes or neither do.

They had agreed that Chris would message Matt and ask him to arrange a meeting in regards to the case, in the meantime Ash would do a few days work for Chris. This would at the very least get him out of the house and give him some money. Ash was not interested in Chris' job, with numbers and accounting being akin to some form of a punishment in hell but he knew it was better than being stuck in the house festering over what might happen. If he was honest with himself, he should not be left alone. They walked out to his car, a white Audi, it was only two years old. As they drove away Ash asked, " So what do you actually want me to do today? I know nothing about accountancy".

"Ha, like I would trust you doing any of that. Eventually you can do data entry and things like that but today I have meeting and errands to run. So keep quiet, listen and learn. If I need anything, I will ask. And don't bloody offend anyone, some of these guys are mighty touchy."

## CHAPTER 12 – THE JOB

They had arrived at a shabby greasy spoon with a dark and gloomy exterior. The front of the building looked wonky to him. Naturally, he had assumed this might be a business deal about buying a derelict building. The windows were papered up to not let any light in and the front door was frosted glass and barely on its hinges. Chris surprised him by getting out and walking straight into the building, wondering if he needed a hard hat, Ash followed him. To his surprise, not only was it a functioning business but there were also customers inside. Not very many, true, but there were some. Gruff dour people staring silently at newspapers or mechanically chasing their beans round the plate, the only bit of life in the place were a group of workmen having a work break.

The owner, a man roughly the size of a fridge, appeared from the kitchen raising his arms in greeting to Chris as he saw him, "Ah Chris, so good to see you. Spot of breakfast?" He asked in a thick Glaswegian accent.
"No thanks Alan, just doing the rounds. I heard you wanted to talk about reconciling the bank accounts, you were struggling with how to account for the new government grant?" As they spoke they walked into the back room, going behind the counter and disappearing from view. Ash went to follow but the woman behind the counter gestured him back telling him to take a seat. He found one suitably far away from the door and sat in the corner. He looked around for a paper but couldn't find one. Chris had insisted he leave his phone behind because in his words, "It's the reason

why your generation can't talk to each other."

It was not good for him to be alone with his brain. Sitting, staring out at the dregs of humanity this café called customers, his mind wandered. Lurking underneath the surface of his thoughts was a primal fear. *It was dread. He was going to prison, he was going to die there.* Like everyone, he had heard the stories. Gangs, drugs, violence and nowhere safe to hide. He was not the sort to go to prison and now realising it was going to happen he knew; he was not the sort of person to go to prison and survive. His parents did not know anything of what was going on. Chris had said they did not need to know. When would they find out? When he went to court? When the newspapers print a headline saying 'ruthless killer behind bars'? Would they visit him? He gave a dark laugh at that. They would not want a killer in their family. No, they would pretend he didn't exist. Erase him and purge him from existence. He lifted his coffee to his lips, drinking mechanically as the dread seeped through him. How long did he think he would last? Would he make the first night? Or would they jump him in the shower? He didn't know how many he could fight off at once, two on a good day, maybe three. His traitorous brain decided that was the time to highlight the fact that he had never been in a fight and would probably run and cry. This was how it was to end, screaming into the dark as nameless criminals ripped him to shreds. He could feel tears welling up and looked around for something to distract him as he felt the panic rise in him.

There were only six customers in the café; a solitary miserable old man who Ash had seen as he walked in, three workmen and a couple gently chatting away. The man had white tufts of hair and looked like he may or may not already be dead, he moved that little. The workmen he could tell were builders or contractors.

They had JMP building on their bright yellow jackets. Two of them were in their twenties, both black with short cropped hair. The other man was obviously the boss, ignoring whatever the other two were talking about and grunting whenever he needed to agree in the conversation. The couple in the corner did not seem that interesting. They both had a mug of tea each and did not look like they were going to eat. *Probably a wise move.* They were wittering on about the latest TV series the other was watching.

And that was how the morning was spent. Chris driving from business to business going in to backrooms or private areas and leaving Ash to spiral about how he was going to survive prison. As they left the dry cleaners and belted up, Ash asked, "What is the point of me coming along?"
"To look, learn and listen, sure you're not doing much at the moment but the point is you are being seen with me. When you go back to them by yourself, they will know you and trust you. Business 101, be friendly, be seen and be known. We will get you a phone and some business cards."

"I thought I wasn't allowed a phone?" Asked Ash.

"You're allowed a work phone. Just not one to play games and ignore people. Listen when you can and for god's sake smile. You look like you're on deathrow." Ash's face paled even more at that. "Pull over, I'm going to be sick," Chris glanced at him, realised he was not joking and pulled the car over.
"Jesus, I didn't think you were this pathetic," said Chris over the sound of Ash vomiting.
"I thought this was only for a few days? I'm either going to be at home or in prison."
"Well forgetting the prison part, what are you going to do at home? You're going to sit at Mum and Dad's until the world hands you something on a plate? What are you going to do for the rest of the

year?" Ash had not thought about this, he just knew he was going to reaudition for university next year. He had not thought that he might need some money in the meantime. "I've got a job all set up for you, and you were told not to leave town until the investigation is finished. So I imagine you're staying."

Ash moaned at this but it made sense. It made a lot more sense when Chris told him how much he was going to be paid for the day.

"£100 a day? Are you kidding me? For sitting down all day? Yes I will take that."

" I thought you might, that money is for you to shut up, play nice and pay attention."

Chris had been contacted by Matt, and they had agreed to swing by his firm's offices. They were modern looking with sleek black windows and silver embossed letters MP and co. Chris had walked him in, instructing the receptionist that Ash was here to see Matt. She had directed him to a luscious leather seat to wait. Chris told him he would get some lunch for the both of them and would be back for an hour. Matt came out striding across the room after only a few minutes. It was the same suit as before. Ash had bets that either the man had seven suits or he slept in them. The lawyer smiled at him and motioned for him to follow. They navigated around the building, finding a meeting room that was available. It was a spacious room with about ten chairs and a mahogany table. It felt much like what he imagined a conference room to look like, he could imagine board members of a big firm making decisions of life and death. He realised that maybe they would make decisions on his life or death in the next few minutes.

Matt sat down at the table and asked Ash, " Do you want a tea or a coffee or anything?"

"No thanks, I'm fine."

"Ok, so Chris said that situations had developed and that you had problems," he carried on in a monotone, "To be precise he said you were hysterically crying all night and sounded like your puppy had just been put down. What happened?"

Ash's face reddened, "I had a bit of news last night, which I did not take very well." He tried to say it in a professional manner like he had seen on tv. Unfortunately, his voice cracked as he spoke. Matt's eyes had narrowed as he was talking, "This would go a lot quicker if you stopped screwing around and actually told me what happened, I haven't got all day."

"Sorry, I was at Nat's house last night."
"That must have been very nice for you, any reason I need to know about your conquests?"

Ash blushed even more. He blurted out before he could be embarrassed anymore, "No, I mean I was there, talking," he gave a meaningful look at Matt as he emphasised his point, "And then the policeman turned up."
"What?" Matt asked, enraged, "Did I not explicitly tell you to bloody call me whenever you have contact with the police?"
"Yes, I know, Nat told him if he was not going to arrest us he should go away or we will put in a claim for harassment. It was about 8:30 by this point."
"Ok," he took a deep breath, "Did you say much else? What did he want?"
"He told us the dick in the coma was getting better and would be available to be questioned next week."
The silence in the room stretched as they both considered the implications of what that might mean. Ash swallowed as he imagined a team of police raiding the office just to come and get him. Matt just continued staring emotionlessly. After some minutes he spoke, "I take it this is a problem for you, as he may be able to

point out you or Ms Carson as suspects?"
Ash's throat had now dried up entirely. He put his hands flat on the table so they would not shake.
"How confidential is this conversation?"
"Totally, just relax and explain the problem. I will keep quiet, don't worry."
"He will know it's us! He will point us straight out. The bastard was trying to hurt Nat, and I hit him. I grabbed something and I hit him. We are so screwed. Jax is going to run to the police and pretend we attacked him for no reason. The police will believe him and we will go straight to prison. I did it after all, should I just pack my bags now?" He was crying again and tried to stem the flow of tears.

Matt had not flinched, or really moved at all as Ash had vented. The only change had been a mild darkening of expression as he pondered the problem.
"It would have obviously been better for everyone if the bloody idiot had not woken up at all, or if you had been honest with the police we could have put in a plea for self-defence and that would have worked out quite well with the prior attack. Or if you just had not talked to them in the first place. How many times do I have to tell people, just say lawyer and shut your mouth. Don't speak at all. Now I know you lied to start off with, and the self-defence option is not possible."
"Why not?"
"Because you told them it was not you, so you changed your story. That's a one way stop to prison my friend."
Ash croaked, "So what the bloody hell are we going to do?"

"You're going to keep your bloody head down. You are going to pretend as if everything is normal and not say a word to the police. I will assume that you will give the same advice to Ms Carson.

Heaven knows I don't need both of you scrambling around creating more issues. I'm sure there are ways to discount his testimony, say he was brain addled or something. One more thing, don't do anything at all. Work for Chris, do not get any ideas about ways to solve this. You know why the policeman came to see you don't you?"

There was silence in the board room as Ash starting trying to breathe normally, "I think so? He was telling us the investigation will be over soon."

Matt laughed, "Something like that, he wanted to spook you. He said it looked like attempted murder with a weapon. He wanted to see if you would hide the weapon etc. Hopefully you did not do anything of the sort and if you did, let's hope you did a good job."

"Oh shit, I didn't think of that," He froze, then started banging his head on the desk.

"Oh for fuck's sake. What is it?"

"It's a metal pole, I threw it away in the alley but I don't know where it is."

"You are really not the sharpest person I have ever met. You will need to get sharper or I won't be able to help you. Do not go looking for this pole, the police will be watching what you do and will have the site locked down. We will just have to hope that they do not find it."

The meeting finished. They left the board room, his secretary handing him some tissues. The tears had stopped but started again at the act of kindness. Matt shook his head and left him, reminding him to "not bloody talk to anyone." The only good part of the meeting was that he had not been told to pack for prison yet. Things looked optimistic as long as he didn't do anything stupid.

Chris took him to a nice little American style diner for lunch . It did burgers, fries, onion rings and not much else. It was nice comforting food. Realising he had not eaten much at all today, he ordered the biggest burger on the menu with the largest coke he could find. Chris surprisingly did the same. Ash raised his eyebrow at his selection but did not say anything. It was quite a busy place with the standard diner playlist in the background; piano jazz from a French elevator somewhere. They spoke about some of the companies that Chris worked for. He seemed to be contracted by most of the companies in the town mostly specialising in local restaurants but did lawyer firms, dry cleaners, shops, insurance companies and building contractors.

"So, Matt was not as pessimistic as you were then?"

"No, he seemed to think it would all be ok as long as both of us don't do anything stupid."

"Have you passed the message on to lovely Nat?" He gave a sardonic smile at that.

"No I haven't."

"Well you best do it then."


They tucked into their food when it arrived. It was hot and filling, and conversation stopped while ate. It allowed Ash to engage in his favourite past time: people watching. It was not intentional but whenever he was in a public place he would just watch. Chris noticed, and smiled, "Always bloody staring aren't you?"

Ash blushed, "It's good for acting, listen to the voices, copy the accents and the walk. Great for improv."

"Yeah that or you're just very nosy."

"Huh, funny. You know I saw those two at the café this morning? Wonder what they do?"

Chris' head jerked up at this.

"Who?" he asked eyes searching. Ash pointed with his hands close to his chest in the direction of where they were.

"Look, the blonde lady and the guy in the red jumper," Ash said.

"Oh I see them, yeah well they must be on a job or something. Eat your burger."

After they had finished their meal, Chris said that he had another meeting with Matt about some business and that I could clock off early. True to his word he pulled out £100 and passed it across the table to him.

"This feels like a drug deal," he laughed, "You do realise this is quite a lot of money."

"I know but you're my nephew, if I can't spoil you, then I can't spoil anyone. And you will earn it in time I'm sure."

Ash pocketed the money. He would usually get about £40 for a shift at the theatre, if that. This was good money and a good job. If he could do this for a few days he would be a rich man, "Same time tomorrow?"

"Absolutely, I knew you would come round. It's the money isn't it?. You could buy the lovely Nat something nice."

"I don't think she would appreciate jewellery from me."

"I was thinking more of a muzzle." Chris smiled.

## CHAPTER 13 – REVELATIONS

Nat had agreed to meet him. In truth, she said she would open the door when he turned up at her house. She then went back to what she had been previously doing; packing.

"What are you doing?" he asked.

"Packing, you idiot. I'm going to go and if you had any sense you would do the same."

She carried on packing as she spoke, rushing to shove all of her clothes in the suitcase. It wouldn't close and she started jumping up and down on it.

"Stop, just stop for a second," he said. She turned to look at him, momentarily, and then resumed her packing. *Nice to know she cared he* thought. "I spoke to the lawyer today, he said to keep on as normal and not to do anything stupid."

"Like what?"

"Like running away?" He gestured to the debris around the room, "If you go, they will arrest me and they will arrest you. You don't want to go to prison, so you're going to leave this and take a breath." Her eyes flashed with anger at him. He held his hands up in an attempt to avoid having more plates thrown at him. Look, you and I both know we need to sit tight. It's been a bloody long day so let's just think for a second?" She stared at him for a while and then nodded ever so slightly. His nerves were in shreds, he couldn't remember a time when they were not. It seemed to be every time he was near this woman his heart was in his mouth and a surge of panic swept through him.

He guided her to the sofa, tentatively, like guiding a rattlesnake. She didn't resist him but he was conscious that there could be a fist or an elbow coming towards him without much warning. As he let her fall to the sofa, she pulled him down with her in an ironlike grip.

Her arms were twisted around his, and her legs around his middle. He could not slink away, so gave in, letting himself fall down with her. It was an awkward landing and he had to try to avoid squashing her as he fell.

As he got comfy, he realised that he had never been this close to Nat. He didn't know what her perfume was but it smelled wonderful. Something of flowers, roses maybe? She still held him tight and nestled her head into his shoulder. Ash thought to make a joke, but then he noticed the tears rolling down her face. His shoulder become damp and then soaked as she continued, going from delicate sniffles to snorts and whines as she sobbed. She had hold of him as hard as she could, coughing with a racking sound, her breath coming in loud sobs. She did not speak, she could not speak, it was all she could do to make sure that she was still breathing. She held onto him and didn't let go.

He didn't remember falling asleep. He remembered desperately trying to avoid pins and needles in his arm but still woke up with numbness. All night he had avoided waking her up, but she had gone without him noticing. The clothes from the night before had been cleared up, the hallway clear from the carnage of the night before. He could smell food now and realised he could hear someone singing. It occurred to him that he may still be dreaming. Following the smell of bacon, he found her in the kitchen.

"Morning," he said as he saw Nat. There was no hint that she had been crying, snoring, drooling or at times all three, during the night. He went to find a mug for coffee. Nat offered no assistance. He was lucky on the third attempt when he had just been ready to give up, with Nat watching and smiling to herself. The mood swing unnerved him and he wondered what was coming next. Pointing to the bacon he spoke, "First class service, bacon in the morning?"

"This is for me. You want it? Cook your own big boy." He eventually found the bacon tucked behind some eggs and then spent the next five minutes looking for bread. "Huh, I didn't think you would know one end of a frying pan from the other," said Nat.

"Yeah some days I can even tie my own shoelaces too, believe it or not."

Under her watchful gaze he attempted to cook. The bacon did not go well. He felt her watching him and all of his culinary skills disappeared under her intent gaze. He put too much oil in the pan, then had the hob on too low. After a while, she turned up the temperature for him, taking pity on him. The overfilled pan spat oil out causing him to let out a little scream and move away. Nat, laughing, took over.

Once he had recovered from the trauma of cooking, and helped with the washing up, he asked her, "So what do you work as?"

" Like I said, I sell my body for money. As we all do, just in different ways."

"Well, that is not helpful in the slightest. Am I not allowed to know?"

"Ok, well what do you work as now? Do you even have a job?" Her face sneered slightly as she said that. Her respect of him was not as high as he thought.

"Well actually, I am working for my... damn it," Ash had stopped short and pulled out his phone.

"What's wrong?"

His uncle answered on the first ring.

"Hello, late on day two? Do you really want this job?" Chris sounded amused.

"Seriously, if you are going to come to work for me you need to be all in. I thought you would at least turn up to work."

"Sorry, I'm at Nat's we got caught up talking about the case."

"I bet you did," he said, still amused, "Well once you get yourself sorted come over to the office. You can walk over and make it in before lunchtime. I know you don't have any decent clothes so that's what we are going to do today."

"We're going shopping?"

"You need a suit, I know a tailor. 12 o'clock ok?"

Ash finished the call, and looked back towards Nat, "Can't believe I forgot work. Not good." He rose to get up and leave. "Well you need a shower first. You can't go in like that."

Ash made a tentative step up to the bathroom. There was a towel helpfully laid out for him, but he didn't have a toothbrush. Today would just have to be a bad breath day. He managed to burn himself a few times before getting the temperature just right and came out smelling of lavender. He could just imagine what Chris was going to say. Getting dressed, he put on the same clothes as the day before. They were clean enough. Nat stopped him before he left.

"Look, I'm not going to run away. Not today anyway, I don't want to give them any more reason to think I'm guilty. But if he wakes up, I'm not sticking around for charges. That gives us a few days at best." She looked at him, wanting him to understand. "Ok, I get it. I really do. I spoke to the lawyer. He seems to think we shouldn't try and hide the pole I hit him with."

"How does he.. you told him? You absolute idiot," Nat hit her head with her palm, "We are screwed now. You've fucked us." She stormed up the stairs and dragged something heavy back down it. It was a suitcase, "You came here last night and pretended all was well and you've ruined everything. You might as well have gone to the police."

"I don't know why you're so angry. At least I'm trying to face this head on. Instead of just running away."

Nat had steadily got redder as he went on. Her hands were shaking with rage and she made sure that he fully understood her next few words by emphasising each one, "Do you remember, that I said I wanted to be a lawyer?" She went on as he nodded, not trusting himself to speak. " Well the super interesting thing about lawyers is that if they think a crime has been committed or have knowledge of a crime, they have to tell the fucking police. Do you understand?"

He stuttered, stumbled over the words and started the sentence again, "But, he asked me. He wanted to know, he said I could tell him and he would keep quiet."

"I bet he fucking did," She laughed, "Now he has you over a barrel. He is going to go straight to the police. I'm going to put my clothes back into the suitcase and go. I don't need to be caught up in this."

"I'm not convinced that you're right, I mean you haven't studied law. So how do you know?"

"I thought it might be handy to work out what to tell lawyers or not. And I found an article. Can you guess what it says? You will not have a duty of confidence if you are being used by a client to perpetrate a fraud, and, by analogy, any other crime." She was

quoting off her phone.
"Ah shit."
"Yes, shit indeed… Now I will hopefully never see you again."

## CHAPTER 14 – ASSURANCES

He could not remember a time when he wasn't panicking. *It seemed his natural state at the moment. Nat's first choice was to run, but where to? They had decided that the police would catch them straight away, so what had changed? Nothing really. If it came to it, he would just plead guilty. At least he would get time off for being honest. Maybe Matt thought they could bargain with information. Did he go straight from his office to the police?* Ash was late to see Chris, so hurried up. His uncle shouting at him, would just add to his day. The plan was to go to Chris' office and from there they would drive to the shopping centre. It was a massive complex of shops, food halls and a cinema. Chris had assured him that he would pay for everything as it counted as a business expense.

"You look like you've just fallen through a hedge. Is this the state she left you in?" Chris asked as he saw him.

" Very funny, I didn't bring a spare pair of clothes."

"After today, I want you to be fully dressed and presentable wherever you spend the night. Also keep a spare change of clothes in the office, or at her house if you are going to be spending more time there."

Ash blushed. Chris set off in the car and they quickly made it off the smaller roads on to a dual carriageway. Ash couldn't wait any longer.

"Chris, I've got an issue. A legal one."

"Well phone your bloody lawyer, that's kind of the reason he talks to you."

"That's the thing though. How can we trust him?"

"I trust him with my life," he looked at him, "Or more specifically I even trust him with yours. This is not a game, I don't care if you like him or not but he is going to keep you out of jail."

"No, I don't mean that. He is lovely. I mean positively angelic.

But I may have made a mistake."

Chris looked at him with a suffering glance and pulled him close, not gently.

"How many bloody mistakes are you making? You need to stop digging, you really do. This is not a playground and if you fuck up any more you are done. No one will be able to save you," Chris' smile had gone now and he was pressed up against Ash's face. "Alright, look at the fucking road."

Chris let go of him and concentrating on the road, drove faster than was safe.

"Well, I just found out that if you tell a lawyer something illegal, they will tell the police. So do you still trust him?" Ash mumbled. The tension in Chris' face released, the car slowed and he laughed, hitting the steering wheel with his hands. It took a few minutes of Chris' wheezing for breath, wiping tears away and when he got his breath back he choked out, "Oh, shut up. He's fine, he won't say a word. Is that what you're worried about? Life is good. The world will end before he says anything. Turn the music up will you?"

After Chris' outburst, he seemed to want to make up for it. Chris sang along to songs in the car and asked Ash about different music he liked. Ash hadn't felt like talking but didn't want to upset his uncle, any more than he already had. As it turned out they both liked Red Hot Chili Peppers, so Chris put it on as loud as his stereo would go. The only words Chris had spoken to Ash about 'the incident' were to make sure that Nat knows and that she didn't do anything stupid. Evidently, Chris expected them both to screw up. The drive took a good 45 minutes and Ash had started to get bored. He had no idea why it was so important for him to have a suit and a change of clothes; the thought had occurred to him that maybe it was for court and Chris was just preparing him.

The shopping centre was much bigger than he had expected. It was called Eastfield and they had had to park in the overflow parking as it was busy. It was built like a huge circus tent in a giant oval. Chris had paced off while Ashley was still staring at it and had to run to keep up with him. They strode past Nike, Adidas, Tommy Hilfiger without looking inside, much to his disappointment. Chris was allowing no detours. They did eventually stop at an EE store for a phone, although Chris picked the cheapest option. He paid in cash. Once done with that they arrived at a suit shop called Top Tailors. There was a young man, in a grey tailored suit there waiting to greet them. He had obviously been told to smile more, as he looked like the muscles in his face were about to burst.

"How can I help you today?" He spoke with energy and went into his sales pitch. When the salesman paused for air, Chris told him to get the owner and to practise his pitch a few more times in the mirror but with less smiles. Ash twitched at that, it did not seem like a very nice comment but it was definitely true. The man had smiled way more than was natural. While they waited Chris wandered through picking out different options for him; definitely not what he would choose for himself. Having never really owned a suit, he always thought the shoes looked ridiculous. Ash pointed out a pair of horrible brown shoes. They looked like something his grandad would have worn to his prom in the fifties, or the ones they automatically give out at an OAP home. Chris looked at him sharply and did not say anything. A much older man came out to greet them dressed in exactly the same shoes Ash had pointed out. It occurred to him that Chris was wearing something similar just in black.

"Hello, dear friend. It's been a while. Any trouble with the suits?"
"No they are just fine, my young nephew here is joining the firm and needs to be shown a sense of style. Can you help him?
"Why of course, you've come to the right place," the old man smiled at them both.

Ash was sized up and put through an array of clothes. He liked the slim fitting suits that he often saw on TV and was told by the old man that those models don't have any style. To his surprise Chris agreed.

"Oh they look good all right, but they look like kids. These suits are meant for business and meant to show that you are a man and not a child of twelve."

Ash didn't believe them but kept his mouth shut. It turned out that Matt and Chris did both get their suits from the same place. It struck him as odd that they did this, and joked that they should probably phone each other to make sure they don't wear the same outfit. No one laughed and Ash stayed in silence after that.

Thankfully, it didn't take long for Ash to get a work suit, trousers and a pack of shirts. He did get a set of the ugly shoes that they all seemed to wear but as for the rest, he felt it looked quite good. This was his first suit, he had never really needed one before. That and he didn't have the money for one. Once they were done with the shopping, they headed back down to the town. When they arrived into the town proper, Chris told him to keep his phone on and then pulled up on the high street.

"I still have a few more errands to run, and I have someone over tonight. Is it possible for you to make yourself scarce?"

"Ooooh, company eh?" Ash give Chris a nudge but the look he received silenced him.

"I think so, can I get some money for a takeout?"

Chris chuckled and passed over another £100.

"You work for a living now, get your own bloody takeaway."

"That's fine, but I need to grab some clothes. I can't do brand new ones every day."

Wondering what to do next, he got out of the car. It was quite easy go to a bar and get drunk. The only one he knew was on the sea front and he definitely did not want to go there. He remembered Stephen's accusing look, so that was a no go, but the lawyers word had stuck in his head all day. What was he going to do when they found the 'weapon'? He knew where it was. It was in the alley towards Nat's house. There had to be a way for him to sort it out and make it disappear. Once they found it, that was it for him. If they did not find it, it would be their word against a psychopath, with a much higher chance of success. He had not thought of where he was walking to until he realised he had been moving towards the alleyway. It was five minutes' walk from where he had been dropped off. Chris had left him by a Nationwide bank, and he had followed the slope of the high street. Everything went downhill towards the centre of the town, then there were hills in every direction apart from towards the seafront. It was 5 o'clock on a weekday and people were flurrying around getting to their homes or quickly trying to finish off some late night shopping as the shops closed. School kids were still walking around in blazers, huddling together playing music with one or two lucky enough to scrape together some money for a costa. Ash strode through, getting quicker as a plan formed in his mind.

He had decided that he would find the pole and dump off the sea. No one would find it. It would be another piece of rubbish amongst the shit of the north sea. The more he thought, the more he realised that the one piece of evidence that would really cause him trouble was this bloody pole. If they couldn't find it, then they couldn't prove a thing. Speeding up, he arrived at the alleyway. Approaching from the road, he could only see the opening with one solitary streetlamp illuminating the surroundings. Looking left, right and behind him, to make sure no one was watching, he turned into the alley and stopped dead. There was police tape and a solitary policeman sitting down on a camp chair with a flask. The policeman looked up and immediately noticed the panic on the 18 year old's face.

"You alright? Alley is off limits, you wouldn't believe the amount of people who try to cut through it."

He recovered from his shock and muttered, "Oh yeah, sorry, you forget sometimes y'know?"

"Where are you going anyway? I haven't seen you before?"

"Oh," Ash saying the only thing he could think of, " my friend Nat's house, I will just go another way."
And with that he walked away.

## CHAPTER 15 – REPARATIONS

"I thought I told you last time, that I hope we never see each other again and that you are a bloody idiot," said a very angry, surprised Nat. She, it was fair to say, was not pleased to see him, although it was a miracle that she hadn't run away yet. The door did not budge as they stood there, eyeing each other.

"Oh, just let me in, you said you wanted to spend more time together." The door opened marginally and he had to squeeze past her and did so as quickly as possible to get out of arms reach. Nat's suitcase was still there by the door, zipped up and ready to go. "Look, I just need somewhere to stay for a couple of hours. You can ignore me etc, I will just watch some TV and stay out of your way. This was your plan remember?

He walked straight in and sat in the living room, flicking on the TV. His shoes came off and he let out a sigh. He ducked as a glass crashed near him.

"Jesus, most normal people throw soft things, like a cushion you know?" He asked, looking around for any more projectiles.

"Well that wouldn't hurt would it?" Nat stalked off to the kitchen, no doubt looking for more things to throw. He waited a few minutes then blurted out.

"I saw a policemen when I cut through the alley," he pitched his voice so she could hear him. She had popped her head round the doorway at that sentence. He heard the kettle boiling and started to panic.

"And why did you go to the alley?"

"I left the thing I hit him with there."

This time it was the coffee cup in her hand that she threw. "Why? Why would you do that?" She took a frenzied step towards him and glass crunched under her feet.

"Because I don't want to go to prison, and that's a one way ticket."

"And so is tampering with evidence at a crime scene you absolute idiot," she shouted, "Next time ask me first if you are going to ruin our lives." Hearing her scream repeatedly at his plan, it was clear to him that she was a psychopath. He hadn't really ever doubted that but her face contorting into rage, nostrils flaring, confirmed it for him. There wasn't a clear escape route out around the glass but he figured if she came with the kettle he would have to risk it, barefoot or not. Taking deep breaths she visibly tried to calm herself. Ash in the meantime started piling cushions as a barricade.
"Put the cushions down you absolute idiot."
"Only if you promise you're not going to throw anything," he said.
"Why do you try and fuck up my life? Why can't you just go and never come back?"
"You literally asked me to be here yesterday?"
She looked around to pick something else up.
"Ok ok," he shouted, "Truce. I will sit here in silence and not say a word. Or better yet, how about we clean up the glass?"
She nodded, handing him a broom. Nat went back into the kitchen, Ash returned to the sofa and his cushion barricade. When Nat returned she snorted seeing him peeking out from his fort.
"You are infuriating, you know that right?" She asked.

"How can I?" he hesitated "How can I make this ok?"
"I really don't think you can," she said, sinking into an armchair, "I think we are royally fucked. I've thought about running but it won't help. They would just catch me anyway and we can't run forever. I would like to have a job and a life at some point. I even thought of turning myself in, or just walking into the sea and just keeping on going."
"What?" he asked shocked.
"Oh get real, only for a second. Prison is better than death."
"How're you so sure?"
"Well if it's not I can die then. The unknown of prison is better than certain death. How's that? Better?"
"You paint a very bright future."
"Well now you have come here, you can go. I am not here for your amusement and we are definitely not friends," she laughed mockingly, "I'm still trying to decide whether you look like the sort of person to be on a register."

"Thanks, well I think you could be a nice person one day if you put your claws away. I have nowhere to go. You said we need to look normal, so I will just stay here. You can do your own thing and I will just play games on my phone or something."

She looked at him with a suffering glance and sighed. "Fine, have a seat and enjoy your Pokemon." She stalked off up the stairs, wine glass in hand. Opening his phone he realised he didn't have much battery as it was and Chris had told him to keep it on. He turned on the TV and flicked through a few channels. After a while, his attention fell to the room around him. There were no personal photos or signs of other people. Ash still didn't have a straight answer on what she did for a living. As time slowly crawled by, his mind kept on coming back to the fact that he could quite easily be in prison in the next few months. How did it work? If you're charged for murder, you probably don't get bail. That meant he would just go straight to prison and stay there. If they found that pole they would know it was him and that would be it. If only that policeman had not been there. Could he go back at night? Would they be able to see him if they snuck by? If anybody found out he could just say he was at Nat's. It could work out perfectly. He knew in his bones that it was just a matter of time before they found it. Could he convince Nat? The problem was, she would fly into another rage or worse, run away. That would let everybody know they were guilty and would leave him holding the rap for everything. No, he decided, it would be much better for everyone involved if he could do it without her knowing. When she was sleeping, he could slip out. Hopefully, there would be a key he could find to let him back in afterwards. Either way, Nat wouldn't snitch on him. She wouldn't know.

He scrolled through his phone, counting down the minutes until it was possible for him to leave without being seen. Ash had been at Nat's house for about 2 hours now, it was coming up to 8 o'clock and she had not come back into the room.

"Nat?" He called upstairs.

"What?" came a bored voice.

"Can I use your toilet?"

Nat appeared at the top of the stairs.

"Don't make a mess," she said and stormed off to her room.

He jumped when he walked back into the living room. Nat was

sitting in the armchair looking at him. It was surprising that she was downstairs, but the part that had scared him was that she was smiling. She did not seem to smile at him often.

"What? Am I not allowed to watch Tv with my new friend?"
"Of course, I'm just not used to smiles. Didn't you call me an idiot earlier?"
" I still stand by that," She continued to smile as she spoke, it looked painful.
"Ok, how about you try your normal face, and we pretend like we are friends?" She dropped her smile and actually looked a little annoyed. "Would you like to play a game? Like twenty questions?" he asked. There was dead silence and then a snort of laughter from Nat.
"You really are ridiculous aren't you. Maybe next we could play musical chairs?"
"What? What is wrong with playing a game."
"I don't know whether you know this but we are adults. Why don't we have a conversation and I will cook us some dinner?"
"Well that does sound better. Now a conversation? Can we have those ground rules back again please? C'mon, tell me what do you do for a living?"
"One day I will tell you."

## CHAPTER 16 – NIGHT TIME ADVENTURES

They talked for a while, but it didn't really mean anything. He had no more ideas about whether she had family, where she grew up or even if she had a flatmate. The one concession he got out of her is that she liked cooking. He had offered to pay for a takeaway but she had refused and was adamant she was going to cook. Nat had given him a few options and they decided on chicken pasta. Nat was going to do some form of homemade pesto, apparently she had worked as a cook in London for a while. Not a chef but a cook, it seemed an important distinction to her anyway.

He helped chop some onions, with the mandatory crying involved as Nat laughed at him. Nat looked through the cupboards, and couldn't find what she was looking for. He tried convincing her that it was fine as it was. She was adamant that she needed to get the ingredients to make it perfect.

"Just go and relax, have a shower, have some wine. I will be back in twenty."

He made some half-hearted protests but realised he might never get a better chance than this. Nat wouldn't know anything, and would say he was at home if anyone asked out of habit anyway. Waiting five minutes until he was sure she was gone, he walked to the alleyway. It was a quick walk but his nerves were on edge. If he saw the policeman he would just have to say he was going home or to the pub. He hadn't quite worked out his story yet, but he would. Last time the policeman had set up from the town side, just off of Cornwall road. If it was only one policeman then surely they would get lazy and just stay there? The policeman had been reading a magazine and didn't seem to interested.

He approached from the seaside part of town, walking as slowly as he could. It was natural to try and speed up and get it over and done with but someone would hear him. He walked past the low front room windows of other people and realised he didn't have his face covered. Would people remember him? He best not get caught, otherwise it would all be over. He stopped just by the alleyway and tried to slow his breathing as much as possible. He held his breath for a count of five, and only ended up coughing and spluttering everywhere. *So much for not making any noise,* he thought. The yellow tape was stretched across the face of the alleyway, he crept under it. Making sure he didn't touch the tape. He knew not to leave fingerprints.

The alley, like all alleys was dark, dingy, and had litter strewn across it. Ash crept, leaning against the wall trying to hide. Realising how stupid he was being creeping round the corner, he changed his walk to that of a drunken stumble. If anyone had seen him creeping, they would have known he was doing something dodgy. That was better, much less likely to look out of place if someone saw him. He had to find the pole; the alleyway wasn't that long and there was nothing in it, so there should not have been an issue finding it. There was a frantic five minutes searching, then a more frenzied time after that, as he still couldn't find it. It was a maddening moment for him, he knew he had dropped it somewhere in the alley. Had the police already found it? Surely not, they would have already taken him away in chains. It wasn't long, metallic and half a metre in length, but it should have been bloody obvious. He had looked in every corner, every part of the floor. Were the police just waiting to see what he did or were they waiting for the guy to wake up and talk? He had looked down but not up. There were bushes to the side, he scrambled to get a look at them. Not caring about noise or thorns, he swept his hand across the foliage. His fingertips brushed something metallic and it made a loud clang as it hit the floor. He swore making even more noise and stuck it under his shirt. Someone shouted at the end of the alley and Ash ran. His hands shook as he held on the pole and his lungs burned in the cold air. He ran down three streets in quick succession and then slowed to a walk, breathing hard. The whole idea was to not look suspicious. He needed to look inconspicuous, he didn't of course, panting for breath. He did have a plan, although it wasn't fully formed yet. More of an outline really. Ash turned towards the seafront once his breathing returned to a vague sense of normal. His nerves were shredded but he knew he had to walk slowly like he was out for a stroll. If he did not get back in time Nat would know that he had gone out, which he had no excuse for. More than that though, he really did not want to get caught with a "weapon" and tampering with evidence. It really would be all over then.

Scrambling down to the shoreline he threw it as far as he could. Breathing a sigh, he sat down and watched it. He had a little laugh, fuelled by underlying hysteria, and decided to wait until it floated away. It didn't. The waves just threw it back at him; he swore and threw it again. This time it fell vertically and dropped straight to the bottom.

It wasn't ideal but would it stay hidden? Would they ever find it? The answer was unfortunate. Yes, they would find it, also anybody who walked in the sea would stumble across it too. *Ah shit,* he thought. He needed a new plan, a way in which to actually get rid of the thing. It was now in more of an obvious place than before, and it would be clear that it had been tampered with. Not only that, he had to go and get the bloody thing. He waded in and grabbed it, laying it on the ground. Being an absolute idiot, he had remained fully dressed. *Real smooth.*

Walking back into town was not an option. Maybe he could bury it in the sand? That also didn't make any sense to him when he thought about. He had tried to dig down as deep as he could and then wondered whether anyone would find it. He imagined some metal detectorist walking along the beach trying to find gold. Plus, how did it look him digging a big hole at night on the beach? There was a solution though, he just had to drop it further into the sea. It was possible to get a boat, but he didn't know how to sail one, or where to get one. If anyone saw him, they would run straight to the police. Even if they reported him for being peculiar, it would not be good for him to get that attention. That left only the pier. With that decision made, he stood and walked back to the promenade, following it as it wound along and then went into the pier. The bar was cold underneath his shirt, it was also wet and covered in sand. It was safe to say his night was not going well. The pier was quite long, about half a mile with a low stone wall either side. He had to stroll past a long fisherman, angling in the cold and a homeless man sleeping on a bench with a Special Brew still in his hand. Ash gave him a quick wave and a smile then winced realising that he wasn't staying inconspicuous. He walked right to the end of the pier, so that he couldn't be seen and dropped it off the side. It rebounded off the wall with a muffled clink before it dropped to the bottom.

(\*\*\*)

Nat walked across the town at a fast pace, head down, avoiding the eye contact of those in the street. A few of the pubs had people outside smoking and she made sure to walk wide of those. She walked past the Tesco's express and was at the bus stop within minutes. The town had a local bus system connecting it with the other towns called the Loop. Not a very imaginative name but it was cheap and the buses were so old and broken that they didn't take card. It was starting to rain a little which made Nat a bit calmer, it gave her a reason to keep her hood up.

She had left the boy at the house, stewing in his own fucking adolescence. He really was no help at all, Nat had been wondering whether to throw any more glass at him when she left but she needed him. She would drop him as soon as she got the chance but he could help her. She needed somebody to alibi her and he would do it. It wouldn't take much convincing, just a mention of jail, of her needing help and he would jump at the opportunity. He really was just a scared little boy. Nat knew what had to be done and he hadn't thought about it at all. Such innocence. He thought tampering with the evidence would sort it out. How would that help? If the sick bastard started talking he would point his finger straight at Nat. Whether the police had a weapon or not, it was pretty damning. No, like always, nobody could see the truth. How does the sick bastard get stopped from talking? Even with no sense left he would be able to point, and she didn't think he could be reasoned with. She could threaten him, but there would always be the possibility that he might turn around one day and say, 'it was her, that bitch did it'. She would always have this cloud over her head, and why? Well because he felt entitled. He felt like he had a right to be a sick bastard. The boy was just as bad, why would she thank him for cancelling out what some other sick fuck did? He had been following her. Hadn't that been just as bad?

No, threatening would not work. There was a solution here and she had decided on it. As always, she was left to make the hard decisions and pick up the pieces.

## CHAPTER 17 – MEETINGS

Ash felt a thrill, a rush. He had done it. No one would find it now, and if they did they would just assume it had fallen off a boat. He waved and smiled to the fisherman and started the five minute walk back to Nat's. The drunk sleeping on the bench had sat up now, and had cracked open another can. He called out as Ash walked past. "Oi, pretty boy. I've seen you before," he grunted.

Ash turned in surprise and then kept on walking, "I don't think so, just a tourist mate." After all it paid to be polite, he didn't want to go through all this hard work to be slashed up by a madman. "Nah, you've been hanging out with her. With Nat." That stopped him in his tracks. The tramp had stood up and walked towards him. Ash backed up, adrenaline flooding his body as he wondered whether to run or not, no doubt he could outrun the thin little homeless man but how did he know Nat?

"How do you know her name? You been stalking?" Ash called out.

"Ah, I know her from old, boy," The tramp said in a gruff voice. "Yeah well that's nice, but I'm going now." Ash backed away not keeping his eyes off the man. He might not be drunk but he had a manic look in his eyes. His beard meshed with his hair and he looked like he hadn't showered for months.

"Ah, I bet she has you involved in some dangerous shit, hasn't she."

"What do you mean?" Ash's breath caught. He was involved in some dangerous shit. *What did the man know?*

The man grunted at his silence, taking it for admittance, "I bet she has you running round after her. Poor Nat always in need of protection? She needed the big man to save her eh? She has done it before and will do it again. She's a killer. Has she branched out and made you a killer too?"

Ash's blood ran cold at the sound of his words. *It hadn't been like that, had it? She hadn't put him up to it, he had just helped her. She couldn't have made the guy attack her could she? No it was madness.* "You're full of crap, I don't know what you're on about." It might have been convincing if his voice didn't come out as a little whine. The man laughed hard.

"Ah, she has you sown up doesn't she? Well let me tell you a story about a boy and a girl. You'll like this one, it has some people you might recognise."

"I'd rather not."

"Well let me tell you, and then you can decide for yourself." Ash tried to move away but the man blocked his path.

"So… boy meets girl. Boy likes girl, girl likes boy and so on. I imagine I don't have to explain that part to you?" He eyed Ash, "No I guess I don't. Anyway, they were in love; so they said. And they did what lovers do, they played, they danced and they sang the night away. Now the boy was an angel. Don't get me wrong the girl seemed lovely too, but the boy was incorruptible. The sort of guy who volunteered on the weekend y'know? Well, they would go out and see the world. She started suggesting different things. She showed him to nightlife and all the things that come with it. This innocent youth, quite like yourself, lapped it all up. She knew this, she whispered and weaved her magic. Suddenly, this angel's halo dimmed slightly. Step by step, we could see this happening and all we ever said drove him further into her grasp. We weren't faultless by any means but we tried everything we could, offered anything for him to get rid of her. He couldn't see the sense of it, not on his life. These whispers became instructions and he followed after everything she did. They were the light and soul of every party. He stopped going to work, stopped volunteering. She had slain the boy and corrupted the man. Though that wasn't enough for a witch like her. She took him deeper and deeper into the world of the depraved. Until one day he didn't come out."

The man stopping talking, looking out to the sea with a grimace. "Well what does that mean?" Ash asked.

"He had another fun night out with the witch. An ambulance was called and they couldn't revive him. Drugs overdose apparently; this from a boy that had never taken drugs in his life. She supplied them, she as good as admitted it. She came in, ruined our boy and then swanned off into the distance. I came to see if I could get the police to do anything around here. Then suddenly I see the same thing on repeat."

"The same thing, she isn't going to kill me."

"No, she might not, but don't tell me you aren't involved in something that could ruin lives. She will kill, when you have outlived your purpose."

"Hang on, I know it's sad. It's awful it really is, but she didn't kill him. He overdosed. That happens."

"I could accept that, hard as it may be. But we had finally got through to him. He was going to leave her, he told us that night that he was going to break it off and come home. Then suddenly he is dead. You can't argue with her, you can't reason with her. Tell me you haven't seen her angry. Tell me you don't think she could do it if she wanted to."

"I... Fuck". The problem was, she could do it. He had no real issue believing that if the moment came she could kill someone if she wanted to. She was formidable. "Right," Ash said, turning away, "This is fun and all but I'm going. Don't bloody follow me."

"Just think on it, think if you're safe," The man said, "You let me know if you change your mind. I will be out here waiting for it to go the same way as last time."

(\*\*\*)

Thankfully, the lights were still out, just how he had left them. He didn't think they would be, she hadn't come back yet. He had made sure the man wasn't following him. It would not be a nice surprise if he had popped up at Nat's house, for either of them. Still, it had him thinking; could she have planned it? Was any of it true? Should he ask Nat if she knows a madman who sleeps rough? Well, he could answer that last question. He wasn't scared of her but it might not be a good idea to ask if she was a malicious murderer.

He took his shoes off and went upstairs, bringing his bag of clothes with him. Where was she anyway? He quickly showered and changed. Drying his hair, he then went back to the living room and put on the TV. Keeping up appearances, he poured a glass of wine and drunk half of it. It needed to seem as if he was fed up waiting and decided to have a drink anyway. Ten minutes into whatever trash there was on the TV, Nat came in with multiple bags in hand.

"I thought you were going to be quick?"

"Decided to do a bigger shop, needed some more food if you're going to come over some more," Nat mumbled, quickly walking into the kitchen. Ash could hear her pottering around and putting things away.

"Do you want a hand?" he asked.

"No, you're fine. Just sit back and relax," Nat said. He thought she sounded odd but didn't get up. He needed to look normal and that was a lot easier when she was in the other room. He waited for a few minutes but hadn't heard anything for a little while, not even bags rustling. She was sat on the floor, head in hands. "What's wrong? What happened?"

"Nothing, don't worry about it."

Nat looked terrible, tears streaming down her face, make up running. Her hands were shaking and she was rocking slightly. "The shopping couldn't have been that bad," he said. Nat didn't reply but continued her rocking. She wouldn't talk. "Can you tell me what's wrong?" Ash asked, feeling helpless. "It's... it's just getting to me. We didn't ask for any of this and here we are. Why us? Why does the world not seem to get any better? It just gets nastier and nastier. Why can't something good happen?"

"The good days will come. There might be worse days ahead but there will be better ones."

She looked up at him for the first time, she even stopped her crying.

"You really are a bloody toddler aren't you? Where did you read that? On the back of a fortune cookie?" Despite her words, she calmed a little.

"Right, bugger off and go and watch Teletubbies or something. I will sort dinner. I hope you didn't drink all the wine."

Half an hour later, dinner was ready. There wasn't much conversation, Ash didn't want to do anything to set her off again and

Nat was mechanically eating in silence. It was a good thing in a way that she was so self-absorbed, he had worried that he would give her a clue about where he had been that night but in her current state she would never notice. So he didn't say anything. When they had finished, he took the plates out and washed them up. By the time he had finished, Nat was asleep on the sofa with the TV still on. He nudged her, to see if he could wake her but there was no chance. There was nothing for it but to lie down on the sofa and see if he could sleep too. She hadn't left much space so he gave up and went to one of the armchairs. He lay there for hours, wondering about what life had in store for them. Was Nat really without any blame in this? Did she start the argument in the club? He had no answers, just a lot of worries. Eventually he slept.

## CHAPTER 18 – INTRUSION

His mind had spent the night conjuring up images of gang tattoos and skinhead cuts, of Nat giving him drugs, of him overdosing, of a maelstrom of situations wherein Nat pointed to the wrong option and each time he followed. When the fitful dreams stopped, being awake was not much better. What did he know about this woman? He had known her for all of two weeks and all she had shown him was violence, anger and rage. The pole was gone now, thank god. So it would make sense for this to be the last night he spent with her. He wanted Nat to like him, she was beautiful and all he could ever dream of. When he first went back to her house, he had imagined her coming back downstairs, undressed and ready for a night of fun. She obviously did not return the sentiment. Plus, it seemed dangerous for his health to be around this woman.

As to whether she had planned it all or not, he doubted it. Even if she were some evil mastermind… What would be the point? She hadn't known that he was following her, and she definitely didn't know whether he would stick up for her. Still, he wouldn't tell Nat about the Tramp. That was a can of worms he didn't want to open.

Round and round his thoughts went. Putting someone in the hospital; did that make him an evil person now? Was he officially a criminal? Never before had he expected to face the prospect of prison. It happened to people, but it didn't happen to him. Would he cry when they sentenced him? Thinking of Nat, he wondered whether she would just refuse any knowledge of the event. She could say it was all him and he had threatened her. It was entirely possible for this to somehow all be his fault. It made sense for him to leave as quick as possible. He would wait until she had woken up, so it would all feel normal, and then go.

Ash got up bleary eyed and took a shower. He started to put his boxers on, in a sleep deprived state, when there was a sound like a gunshot. Stumbling, he fell, with one leg in and one leg out. There were shouts on the stairs and a banging on the bathroom door. He shouted, "I'm coming, I'm coming," when he recognised shouts of "Police". The door splintered inwards, and Ash barely covered was dragged out and cuffed. From the screams downstairs, Nat had been similarly grabbed. Ash shouted at anybody who would listen. Asking them what they were doing, what was happening. Nobody answered him.

"Can you at least bring my clothes?"

A policeman, ignoring his protestations and pushed him outside. Ash could only make sure that he had covered himself properly as they bent his head and put him in the back of a police car.

In his dazed state, it took a while to realise the magnitude of the situation. It seemed they weren't just going for a chat. The two police officers only spoke to him to read him his rights. "Ashley Merson you are under arrest on the suspicion of murder. You do not have to say anything but it may harm your defence if you do not mention when questioned something which you later rely on in court. Anything you do say may be given in evidence."

## CHAPTER 19 – TROUBLE

The cell was surprisingly clean. He had expected a dark, dank room with vomit on the floor and a murderer in the cell with him. They had put him alone, gently but firmly steering him towards the cell and closing the door. There was no time given for when he would be interviewed, not that it would be much help as there was no clock in the room either. There was a comfortless bench which Ash sat on. It had some sort of mattress but it was a mattress in name only. It was rock solid.

He had always heard isolation was tricky, and that some lawyers called it inhumane. He hadn't really understood what the fuss was all about. It was just time alone in your own thoughts. If anything there were no annoyances, no frustrations from the outside world. Surely he would feel safe here?

Ash held to that belief for around an hour. He didn't know if it was an hour, or a day. He could hear the clattering of people's boots outside and doors shutting but rarely voices. When he could hear voices, it was a mumble here or a mumble there. Nothing distinguishable. He knew there had to be a purpose to why they put him in here. Getting him to simmer in his own thoughts. They must be thinking that he would panic, and worry about what they knew and what would happen to him. It was working. Ash had nothing to think about apart from the situation he was in. Maybe he had been caught walking to the beach, or perhaps they found DNA on him at the crime scene. Maybe yesterday had truly been his last day as a free man. He tried to clear his mind from the stress and anxiety that was threatening to drown him. Naturally, it did not work. Reassuring himself, he tried thinking of things that were definite. His lawyer was coming, and he was going to be interviewed. In here he was safe, he only had to deal with his brain, just had to endure until Matt saved him. Something electrical was humming nearby; it had been there when he had come in, but now he could feel it. Walking round

## The Girl Who Laughed At Birds

the room, he tried to isolate the sound. Where was it coming from? Was it in the room? No, it couldn't be.

Sitting down worked for a short while, then he resorted to striding across the room. It was tiny. There was nothing in it but the spongy blue mattress less than an inch thick. It reminded him of his gym mats at school. Something must have changed for him to be arrested. They were free to go all this time and suddenly the police came in to Nat's house; not just a polite knock at the door either. They had barged in and come running with handcuffs. He hit his head against the wall at the realisation of his own stupidity. The obvious reason being that the man he had hit must have woken up and described Nat. That must have led them to Ash. He had put himself with her in the police's eyes. He was amazed it took him so long to realise it. It was their word against his. It was obvious there was a fight at the club. Did it look like a revenge attack? If so, by who? Clearly, him. On and on his thoughts spiraled.

Thankfully, he did have some human interaction between his cycles of restlessness, panic and restless panic. The only reason he knew that the hours had ticked by was a man coming to check on him every hour. The man who had signed him in, the 'Custody Officer' or something, had read out his rights of what he was entitled to: "A private consultation with a lawyer", "informing someone you have been arrested" and " a look at codes of practice". Ash had almost taken up the offer on the codes of practice to occupy himself but had decided against it. Then it hit him. They did not say attempted murder, or GBH. They had said murder. The guy was dead. He sunk to the floor, eyes closed, trying his hardest not to cry. Ash was in some serious trouble. He knew it, they knew it. A man was dead and they had him in the cells already. It was a open and shut case.

When Matt arrived, with a policeman opening the door for him, he stepped in and looked at the pitiful wreck that was Ash. Despite his best efforts, he had cried and not stopped. He had been mourning the life he would never get to have. At times he had banged on the walls, and he had stopped trying to be quiet after the dam had been broken. What was the point? If this is how it was going to end, then what did it matter?

Matt looked him up and down in a stern manner. There was a

clear disparity between the cool, collected manner in which he held himself and Ash's utterly dishevelled state.

"Up you get, don't say anything," said Matt. They were led to a separate room across the station, Ash's eyes struggled to adjust to the light and noise, but he didn't say anything. Keeping his head down, he stared at the floor not wanting to look at the lawyer. The lawyer spoke without emotion, "I didn't realise you were a complete pussy."

At that, Ash's head lifted sharply and he opened his mouth to speak but Matt forestalled him with a smile, "Ah good, I thought you had totally cracked."

"They have me on murder. I'm screwed."

"Not necessarily, the unfortunate victim," Ash winced at that, "The unfortunate victim died last night at 11pm. A drug overdose, heroin most likely. Quite hard for someone to score when they are in hospital don't you think? So he was poisoned. They have arrested you because you two are the most likely candidates, stupid enough to do it and with enough motive to stumble into doing something unforgivably dim."

Ash stared at him open mouthed. *Poison? Who poisons people?* "So... Someone else killed him?"

Matt burst into laughter, it took him a good couple of minutes to recover as he wiped his eyes.

"Well, I can't say I didn't hope that would be your take on it but you don't have to sound so shocked. Now you have an interview coming up, here's what you do."

## CHAPTER 20 – TWO OPTIONS

The interview room was more comfortable than he was expecting. Ash had watched way too many police shows, the American ones where they were always screaming and shouting. Sometimes they threw things. Matt had reassured him that if anything like that happened the case would be thrown out immediately.

"Now Ashley, we are part of the murder investigation team, and you are under arrest on the suspicion of conspiracy to murder. Do you understand this charge?"

He looked at Matt quickly, and then nodded.

"Ok, I am going to ask you a few questions now," She took a card out and read from it, "You do not have to say anything. But, it may harm your defence if you do not mention now, something which you later rely on in court. Anything you do say may be given in evidence. Do you understand?"

Again, Ash nodded.

"Could you confirm verbally for the recording please?"

Ash nodded. The policeman looked at him expectantly. "Oh right, yes, yes I understand," He blushed.

"So Ashley, where were you last night?"

"At Nat's house, with Nat."

"So, you are saying that last night you and Natalie Carson were together, correct?"

"Yes."

"And did you spend all of last night together? Did either of you go out at all last night?"

Ash paused. *Shit.* What should he say? He had already hesitated for too long. They knew now that he had hesitated. Why had he? Oh crap.

"Yes, that's correct."

The policeman leant forward on his chair, "That's interesting, can you tell us why it took you so long to come up with an answer. Surely, you know where you were last night and what happened? You can't be that forgetful."

Sweat was pouring down Ash's face as he sipped the glass of water they had provided.

"I think I may need a break. That's allowed isn't it?"
"Of course, but we have just started. Is there anything the matter?" Matt stepped in at this point, " I need fifteen minutes break, while I talk with my client."

(\*\*\*)

Nat swore. It felt good. It felt right. Sometimes just picking the right one really hit the spot. She didn't scream it at anyone in particular. After being surprised by the police, she had gone quietly. And now this smarmy idiot was trying to ingratiate herself with her. "So Nat, I would like to make your life easy. I'm not going to shout, or demand you tell me. That man, Jax, wasn't very nice to you was he? He attacked you, he made you mad. He made you angry, and you decided to end him. You decided to get rid of him, to make life easier for you. Isn't that the truth?"

Nat said nothing, just stared off into the distance. Damn, this would have been much easier with a cigarette. She imagined Ash would be in tears by now, probably screaming for his parents to come and save him. She had asked after him, if only to see whether he would break down and tell them everything. Matt had been true to his word and brought another lawyer, a stone faced woman who essentially boiled down her advice to, "They are searching your house now, if you haven't left any evidence at your house, the burden of proof is on them. So shut up until anything changes." *Nice to know her lawyer trusted in her innocence.* As much as she didn't want the help, Nat could see that it was good advice, so apart from the initial outpouring of foul language she had refused to even say no comment. At times they seemed to want to check if she was competent and that she understood the language. When this happened, she gave them a stare and nodded her assent. And the interview rolled on and on.

(***)

"My client has answered the same question three times, can we move on?" Asked the lawyer. Matt was unflustered at the repeated attempts from the officers to trip up his client. If anything, he looked bored. It was clear to him that the officers were going round in circles.
Ash's sweat issue had grown so bad, that in other situation he would have asked for a shower and a change of clothes. The police by contrast were looking comfortable and Matt himself was not showing a drop of perspiration.
"Yes, and as you know we can ask as many questions as we like. It is up to Ashley here to answer them. And he did a particularly bad job on that first one."
"Do you know what the definition of insanity is officer?" Matt spoke up. The officer smiled at that but Ash didn't understand it. *What did that mean?*
"Yes, I do. But if we find out Mr Merson has been lying, would you like to explain to your client what that would do for him at trial? It would really colour the jury's opinion if he had to retract, recount or say that he had made up part of his testimony."
With that Matt went quiet. Ash was still trying to work out what to do. Nat had left during the night, and she had been gone a long time. He had been gone for over an hour and she still wasn't back when he had returned. Nat said she had gone shopping, but it simply didn't take that long. It hadn't occurred to him, but when the police asked if she had time to get to the hospital and back, it dawned on him. She did. *Could she have done it?* Nat suddenly had decided not to run away, had let him in, despite her protests. She knew he would cover for her, because well he had already lied in the past. He could not come clean now because he would be known as a liar and they would ruin him for it. The more he thought about it, the more it made sense. What had the tramp said? Don't you think she could kill someone? He was convinced now, he knew for sure she could. He was increasingly sure now that she probably did. Where did that leave him?

(\*\*\*)

Nat's patience was slowly disappearing as the smarmy man continued his drivel, trying to make friends with her. She presumed he must always be this slimy. How did his colleague feel about it? She hadn't opened her mouth at all, at the very least she had the grace to look a little embarrassed at the man's monologue. It wasn't the same man that had knocked on her door a while ago, he didn't have the same composure. This guy in front of her was a weed. Inconsequential, she almost opened her mouth to tell him that and then closed it again, reminding herself that animosity here would not go in her favour.

The absolute idiot of a man saw her slip and thought he was onto something. He redoubled his efforts, dribbling more senseless nonsense, falling over himself to spew more bullshit. Nat rolled her eyes at him and then nodded at her lawyer, to indicate that it was time for a break.

When the meeting resumed, the irritating idiot had been replaced. She knew the man who stood before her and introduced himself to the tape as DCI Heath. He did not offer his hand in greeting. A terse man, who grunted a few sentences to recommence the interview and then stopped talking. *Thank god,* Nat thought. Anything to not hear the other one's drivel.

"Nat, I don't think you understand what's going on here," the woman police officer said, her name was Taylor, Nat thought, "There are two investigations open. There is a murder from last night, which we are interviewing you in regards to, but you are forgetting about the night where the victim was hospitalised in the first place. You have been listed as a key suspect for both. If you are connected in either you will be convicted, and you will probably be convicted of both if you can't provide yourself with better alibi's. Mr Merson, as your likely accomplice will be convicted too. If we find any evidence of a murder weapon, or disprove any alibis, you will be charged immediately and that is it." She spoke in a soft manner, and her voice was calming. She wasn't speaking inane nonsense. It actually seemed to Nat like she was being genuine. *Blind fool,* Nat thought. "In the next room, my colleagues are interviewing Mr Merson. Now I don't know what happened, but I am here to help you. What do you think they are talking about in the next room? Do you think Ashley will do as well with the stone faced silent treatment? Do you thinking he is panicking about prison? This is big boy stuff, do you really think he can handle this?"

This caught Nat's attention. For the first time in the interview, she felt a wave of panic rush through her. Taylor had seen her eye contact, how she had reacted. She pushed forward her advantage. "Now, I'm sure none of this was your idea. You never wanted to hurt anyone. You were the victim here, you were harassed. You fought back when you had to. Now, Ash, he wanted to impress you and he attacked the victim. He probably meant to scare him, didn't realise how easy it is to hurt people. He then made you shut up about it. He pressured you into not saying anything. You've lied, you're scared. Let me help you, we are happy to strike a deal with you. We can clear you of all charges if you just tell us what happened. If you tell us what Ashley did."

## CHAPTER 21 – THE BOUGH BREAKS

"I can see you sweating, son. You're in over your head and we know it. We can add obstruction of justice to your paperwork if you like. We have you on tape lying, and we know you're lying. So when we find out what happened, you're in a world of trouble."
Ash had been in a panic for the last hour. Willing himself to be silent after his first few sentence went to absolute crap. Matt had talked to him over the breaks, reassuring him, coaxing him back to the interview room, shouting at him when he refused. In the last break, Matt had told him that he could either accept his advice as a lawyer, or go and hang himself alone. It was the lawyer's opinion that the only way out of this, was to keep quiet and provide an alibi or give them some information to keep him off his back, his words were: keep to the truth or don't say anything. He had then instructed Ash to not have any more breaks, it was showing the wrong impression and quite frankly, if they didn't think Ash was guilty they would do now after his woeful performance.

DC Rexham now continued his obsession of their whereabouts last night. Ash had his palms face down on the table to stop his hands shaking, though his fingers were twitching now. "See, we police officers are trained in interrogation. We are trained to look for chinks in the armour. What do you think I can see about you? No? Well I can tell you. You're in over your head, you've been dragged into a situation out of your control. Your lawyer will tell you, if this goes badly for you, you will be charged with first degree murder and whatever I can throw at you. Now this is god's honest truth, the worst case scenario is life in prison. Tell me that's not true Mr lawyer?"

Matt gave a sigh and looked at the officer, "Yes, the worst case scenario is true, although unlikely. We are a long way away from even deciding on whether to charge my client or not."

"True," Rexham nodded, "But out of your own lawyer's mouth Mr

Merson. That is a possibility. And you are doing all of this for what? I know you didn't mean for any of this to happen. You're not a cold blooded killer. What did you want to do with your life?"

"An actor," Ash choked out. The policeman smiled.

"You see? And yet you're here staring at the barrel of a life sentence. I just want to know what happened? How did you get involved? If you give me something, if you tell me how all these pieces interlink, I can show leniency, I can let you off. Will you help me, to help you? How does leaving this cell today sound? No culpability, no blame. You tell me what happened, and you can carry on with your life. You can be free to act on whatever stage you wish. I mean, what does Nat mean to you? What do you owe her? She dragged you into this. She did all of this, a woman you barely know. Did you know she was a suspect before? Implicated in a drug overdose? This is her M.O. She has a record. You don't. You're innocent. Don't get dragged down with her."

Ash stared at the man. So it was true. She really had done it. "What do you say Ashley? She is dangerous. She has done this before and we never caught her. Now she has done it again and we have the chance to put her away for good. What do you owe her?"

(\*\*\*)

Overall, she did not rate the experience of being locked up. At least she had a toilet and they had given her some food. Nat had even thought about exercising, but not even the threat of a prison sentence would have got her to start doing press-ups. Looking back on her interview, she had given them nothing. The weedy little fucker had offered her cigarettes and she did not even look up, it had taken all of her willpower but she wouldn't have taken anything from the little shit.

The more she listened to their questions, the more it was obvious they were fishing for information. She had thought Jax had identified her or they had some vital new evidence but it was the same few things said on repeat. *"Where were you? Did you kill him? Did Ash make you keep quiet? You're going to spend forever in jail, do you know that?"* Sometimes they didn't even finish the first question before going on to the next. She couldn't believe that demanding people to tell their secrets actually ever worked. Still, thank god, they switched interrogators halfway through. She may well have stabbed him given half the chance. It was possible to put in complaints against police officers and she floated the idea to her lawyer who gave her an eye roll. Thinking back, it probably was not the right time to do it, in the middle of the interview.

It was very possible that she heard Ash screaming at one point. In one of the other cells, there had been a person crying and banging on the walls. She could believe the crying, but if he banged on the walls he would snap like a twig. It almost offended her that they thought her so weak as to be controlled by him. He was probably calling out for his parents as soon as the handcuffs came on. DCI Heath wanted to know whether he was using sex to control her. As if, she would probably have to draw him a picture to get the idea. Even the possibility of that made her skin crawl. He probably had hidden cameras in his clothes.

Nat paused her pacing and thought about it for a moment. That was probably a bit too harsh. Ash was an idiot of epic proportions but for all his faults he was sincere. When the interview had finished and they steered her back to the cell, the woman who had so softly questioned her had said, "Just give him up, for your sake, don't throw away your life because of a mistake he made."

The police had imagined all these situations for her, of how a girl like Nat would find it tough in prison. That she, *'might never see the light of day if she said nothing'*. It was more rubbish from people that didn't care. They did not want to help her, not really. They just wanted a name to put on paper, to take to court, to send to prison. They wanted to hammer a nail and they didn't much care who it was. They had put Ash up on a platter for her. *'Just say the word and we will charge him,'* they said, *'You will be free to go.'* Well that wasn't how she did things. Yes, he had put the bastard in hospital, but he had done it to save her. He had been fair, despite her best efforts, she did not hate him. It surprised her, but the more she thought about it the more she realised it was true. She didn't necessarily like him, but he wasn't the absolute scumbag she usually met. She wouldn't give him up to save herself. It just wasn't something she could do.

There was a bang on her door and the inspectors were back in full force. When they brought her back in this time, it was DCI Heath and the weedy fucker. Her lawyer had returned and in the interim had said that the police seemed to have found something. Nat had no idea but if it was anything like all of their other information, it was crap. They couldn't have found anything in the house, and she highly doubted anybody had seen her yesterday. That left Ash. What had he said?

"So, new information has come up, information that puts a different focus on our questioning. Your friend was very talkative, and gave us the information we needed. We know you killed Jack Hawkins. You are a murderer, and now we have a witness that ruins your alibi."

Nat looked calmly at the two of them and laughed. They seemed so smug, so righteous that they had it all worked out. She had thought that Heath was alright, if sanctimonious, but evidently he was as stupid as the lot of them.

"Is this your big reveal? Shouldn't you have had confetti or trumpets or some shit? You got nothing, more than that…" She spat as she spoke, "I bet he didn't give you shit. You're making it all up."

"Nat," interjected her lawyer in a warning tone. Nat stopped talking. "We have more than nothing, I assure you. Someone injected a serious amount of heroin, enough for the victim to overdose. That's your style, we know that from your history. You can't alibi yourself, as your sweet friend Ash said you took an hour to go shopping down the road. You knew he was going to wake up, because you were informed. So there is means, motive and weapon. It's looking pretty damning. So do you mind telling us where you were when you left the house last night?"

A tear left Nat's eye. She thought she was past that, she had done all her crying before and promised herself she wouldn't do it over people that didn't matter anymore. *Her style?* She raised a shaky hand to wipe away her tears. DCI Heath continued to question her. "Are you going to tell us why you killed him now?"

*Why had he betrayed her? Why had he given her up? She had trusted him.* Yet another slime ball who had let her down. She knew he was a scared little boy, he had shown that more than once. Maybe, he just wanted to save his own skin. I mean self-preservation was not an entirely new concept to her, it's just Ash didn't ever seem like that sort of person. He was a sappy idiot, but he wouldn't have betrayed her. He would have wanted to protect her, to save her. There was only one reason why he would do what he did. He believed she was a killer.

"No comment."

(\*\*\*)

Ash couldn't help it. When they told him that he was free to go, he smiled. He laughed, hugged his lawyer and almost tried to high five the officer talking to him. Matt put his hands on Ash and manhandled him out of the door. As they broke into the sunshine, Ash spotted Chris outside and ran towards him. Chris laughed when he saw Ash's happiness but Matt hurried over scowling. "Don't be an idiot. Calm down. Stop smiling," He hissed. Ash tried to stop smiling but he couldn't do it.

"What does it matter," Ash said, "They let me go."

"Yes, they did. You however, are not meant to act surprised that you're innocent. You are not meant to high five officers as if you literally just got away with murder."

Ash's smile faltered. Yet again, Matt was right. Chris shook hands with Matt, promising to meet up soon and then the lawyer drove away. Chris motioned to him.

"Well are you going to get in or what?"

The car was silent for a minute and then Ash let out a breath of relief. His hands still shook but he was free. The cloud over his head had gone. His life was his own again. He wasn't going to spend the rest of his life in prison. The idea that his life had been that close to slipping away, hit him hard. Tears flowed and he couldn't stop them. Chris didn't look at him but waited for him to get a handle on his emotions.

"It's good to have you back," Chris said, once Ash had composed himself. He pulled away, quietly joining the traffic. "So where are we going?" Said Ash, realising that Chris was not taking the route home.

"We are going to celebrate," shouted Chris, beeping his horn as he did so.

"But Matt said to keep our heads down and pretend that we expected nothing else."

"Yeah, well he would say that, myself, this is another day where we are alive and the world hasn't ended. You've been given a pass Ash. How could we not celebrate?"

They made their way to a fancy Italian restaurant, no doubt it was another one of the business' he "looked after". The manager greeted him at the door by name and brought them to their seats. Chris ordered a bottle of champagne and toasted Ash's release. They ordered as much as they could from the menu and gorged themselves until they were full. Chris turned serious for a moment as the waiter cleared away their table.

"I knew you didn't do it y'know. You're a good kid, not the type to kill in cold blood. Always knew they would let you go," he smiled warmly at Ash.

"I'm glad someone did. I knew I didn't kill him, but when they talk to you it feels like you did it all. Feels like you should confess to everything whether you did it or not." Chris gave a snort and took a sip of his drink.

"I know exactly what you mean. I got stuck in a queue with a police officer the other day, felt like I had five kilos of coke up my ass." Ash spat out his drink all over the table. The two tables near him glared, some of the champagne mist might have hit them too. "Matt said you held up well under interrogation," Chris said.

"I think you must have misunderstood him. I cracked almost immediately. I think I cried longer than I held it to together," Ash chuckled.

"He did mention the tears," Chris gave Ash a wry look, "You will have to get over that someday but that will come in time. He said apart from the first slip up you were fine. You didn't panic when they presented you with life in prison. In the end, you put suspicion onto some else and helped the police rule you out. That's a tick in my book."

"I think he made it sound much better than it actually was. Anyway, I know I didn't do it. It must have been Nat. They would have worked it out eventually."

"What makes you say that?" Asked Chris. Ash paused, wondering how much to say.

"She left for over an hour last night. When she came back, she was crying her eyes out as if something awful had happened. Then suddenly the guy is dead. Doesn't take a genius to work it out does it?"

"No, that's true," Chris admitted.

"And it turns out," Ash continued, "She has done it before. Some boyfriend she knew died of a drug overdose."

"Yeah, doesn't mean she is a killer."

"Police assumed it was her but didn't have enough evidence. It all seems to add up though doesn't it?"

"Yeah, I guess it does. She is quite a loose cannon. I wouldn't want her mad at me. I take it you're not going to see her anymore then?"

Ash looked at him dumbfounded, "She is at the police station, about to be convicted of murder. It's not likely we are going to be pen pals is it?"

"Not according to Matt, she just got let out."

"What?" Asked Ash. He had raised his voice so loud the waiters were looking at him. He leant closer and lowered his voice, and repeated, "What?"

"Yeah, he just said CCTV cleared her. So you're both free. Happy endings all round."

"But how could they let her go? They know it's her."

"Apparently not," they lapsed into silence. Ash swore. *When she got out she would be furious with him. The police would have told her by now. What would she do? More to the point, why did they let her go? It must have been a technicality. Maybe they were letting her go to gather more evidence. Ash was certain now. It must have been her. She was the only one apart from him that had anything to lose. That means the police had just let a killer on the loose. By the sounds of it, for the second time. It might even be him next. How angry would she be with him, knowing that he had betrayed her? She had already shown a violent streak, would he be next on her list?*

Ash returned his attention to Chris. He wasn't as excited and happy as he was before, "So, what happens now?"

"Tomorrow, you are going to work for me and start to pay off the time I have invested in you, but today we celebrate." They ordered extras of everything. Ash had so much dessert he felt like he would be sick, and Matt had to ask for a glass of water after drinking too many glasses of wine. Ash's phone beeped; it was a text from Nat.

*I think we should talk.*

Ash's head was a little fuzzy but he knew that the only thing he was certain of was that he should not be in a room alone with Nat. It wouldn't be safe. He replied:

*Sure, not tonight though. I will let you know what day I can do. What do you want to talk about?*

He waited, and eventually the reply came:

*I will tell you when I see you. Let me know when you can meet. Don't avoid me.*

God, she scared him. They ended up taking a taxi home with Chris leaving his car at the restaurant. Ash was petrified of Nat, and he didn't know what to do with her. The police wouldn't be much help, he had only just cleared himself after all. Chris was no help. Ash looked to Chris who was drooling on the sofa, snoring very loudly. Ash walked to his bedroom and settled down to sleep. He managed to put Nat out of his mind, she was a problem for another day. Falling asleep a free man for the first time in a long time.

## CHAPTER 22 – THE HANGOVER

Ash awoke with a pounding head. It took him a while to realise where he was, in his own bed, still free. Seeing the debris cluttered around the room, it was clear that he had had trouble getting into his bed without knocking everything over. He picked up his bedside lamp, that was a casualty of the night before, and slowly crawled to an upright position. His brain felt like they had been chopped up, scrambled and then stuck in a blender. Staggering out of his bedroom, he went in search of coffee. The kitchen was filled with the smell of eggs, the stench of Chris cooking an omelette flowed into his nostrils. Coughing, he ran to the bathroom to be sick. How could he have eggs with a hangover? He must have felt worse than Ash had. Ash finally returned from the bathroom, out of breath and feeling revolting. Chris was sitting waiting for him, a cup of coffee on the table, happily munching away on his omelette. *Sick bastard.* Ash pushed himself to eat some dried toast, he made it halfway through and just threw it away. He wasn't ready for that yet. A wave of nausea rolled over him as he sat down, trying to focus on Chris. "How, did you manage to eat that… I can't even say the word. Just smelling it almost killed me."

"You kids, bloody amateurs the lot of you," he was grinning at him, getting some form of pleasure from tormenting him, "I could name other foods that might set you off if you like, kippers and custard, sardines, tuna, three day old kebab." Ash spluttered and ran back to the bathroom, with Chris cackling in the background. "I want you showered and ready in half an hour. It's time to work for you money."

An hour later, they were in the car heading to their first dropoff. They only had to stop twice for Ash to be sick. Once he wiped the sick away, he took a mint from Chris and tried to understand what he was saying.

"So you're telling me, I go into this dry cleaners, say I'm from Techsom accounting, and I work for you. And they will just give me 3 grand?"

"Boy, don't be an idiot. We do their accounting, which means when they need to pay into their bank, we do the leg work."

"I thought everything was done online nowadays."

"Yes but not for cash businesses you idiot. Pay it into this bank account number." He handed Ash a slip.

"Surely they could just do it themselves?"

"I will say this once, and once only. We have a set way of doing things, do not mess up, do not take anything, do not offend anyone and for god's sake do not mention anything we do to anyone but me."

Ash strolled into the dry cleaners. There were a couple of customers queuing, and he waited for them to be served. It was hot in the dry cleaners, he could hear tumble dryers going. Well he assumed they were tumble dryers, he didn't really know or care what equipment they used. When the customers had gone, he walked up to the counter. He desperately hoped he wasn't going to be sick all over them.

"Hi, My name is Ash. I am from Techsom accountancy. I'm here to pick up the weekly delivery."

The woman looked at him oddly. "I've not seen you before," she said passing over a rucksack.

"Never been here before. No fancy briefcase?"

"You'll learn. Off you go."

Ash made three more pick-ups that day. Each time he went to a different bank and paid in the amount to a different person. Ash didn't really think much of it, although was sure that these businesses could just go to the bank themselves. Maybe it was just first class service from Chris' company. Chris drove him to each site, stayed in the car and then drove him to each bank. He must have wanted to make sure that Ash didn't get any accounts wrong. When he had driven Ash to the bank the first time, he made it clear to Ash, "Do not tell the bank teller that you are doing lots of deliveries of money. You don't want someone to hear you, might make you an easier target to rob."

As the day wore on, Ash recovered from his dreadful hangover. He started to feel more functional, and asked more questions. What was his job title? Chris told him that he was now a courier. He would move items, move money and work as a liaison between businesses. By the time it got to one o'clock, Chris showed him that he meant exactly what he said. They had arrived at a big warehouse on an industrial estate. They drove past a couple of builders' merchants and even a brewery to get to a dusty warehouse at the back of the estate. It didn't have any cars in front of it and they entered through a side door. Chris inputted the key code to deactivate the alarm but sheltered the code from his view. He obviously didn't want Ash to know, and that was fine by him. No responsibility if something went wrong. The warehouse was deceptively big and half full with different sorts of items. There were boxes of electrical goods, some foodstuffs, forklift trucks, beer barrels and even a lorry waiting to be loaded.

"Right, I have a few meetings. I need you to load this lorry. Don't use the forklift, you're more likely to poke a hole in the wall. Stack those boxes," Chris said pointing to the boxes full of TVs and laptop, "Stack them floor to ceiling. Don't break anything, don't look in any of the boxes. Call me if anything goes wrong." And with that he left.

Luckily, Ash had brought his earphones and put some music on his phone. Otherwise, it would have been earth shatteringly boring. The boxes were heavier than he expected, and it took time but he was making good progress. Chris hadn't told him how long it should take him or when he would be back. It took him hours, but he was proud of the job he had done. He had stacked the boxes neatly, and managed to fit them all in. He was covered in sweat, no doubt some of it was also alcohol leaving his system. He sat down on a concrete lip of the loading bay. If he had to do this on a daily basis he might actually gain some muscle from this job. His arms ached, as did his legs.

"Who are you?" growled a man walking in from another door Ash hadn't seen. Ash jumped, pulling out his headphones and standing up, stuttering. The man was huge with tribal tattoos along his arms and along his neck. "What are you doing here?" The giant repeated himself, and Ash realised that far from being friendly, the man was walking towards him menacingly. Ash put up his hands and moved backwards.

"I'm just stacking some boxes, like I got told." As he stepped closer, Ash backed up around the lorry, giving himself as much space as possible.

"I'm working for my uncle Chris. He told me to just stack the lorry up." The man paused, obviously trying to work out whether Ash was telling the truth or not.

"Alright, but I'm going to phone him. If he says he doesn't know who you are, you're not going to like it."

Ash nodded, wondering just how much time it would take for him to get to the door and run away. With a twisted smile, he then pulled out his phone and dialled a number. He mumbled into the phone a few times, saying things like "ok", "alright" and "of course". When he finished the phone call he turned to look at Ash, his eyes full of fury.

"Interesting call, said they don't know who you are". And with that the man ran at Ash. Ash screamed and ran away. He didn't know where the doors in the warehouse led to, it could be a trap. Mind reeling, Ash tried to think of where he could go. Moving around the lorry, he managed to put some distance between himself and the madman now screaming at him. If he ran all the way around, the psychopath might just be waiting for him. Escaping was the only thing on his mind but he couldn't find a way to do it. There were no exits that he could trust. His only other option was to hide. There were boxes everywhere, could he open one up and get inside? No, there wasn't enough time. He ducked behind the forklift to give him some more time. The longer he spent without getting spotted would be better for him. The man was still shouting, he had walked past the lorry and was looking around the frozen food area. He was swiping at things, straining to listen, trying to catch any sound or sight of Ash. Ash breathed in deeply and ran for the only place of safety he knew moving into the back of the lorry he had filled and pulled the shutter down behind him. The man would hear him, but he couldn't get to him. He got his phone out of his pocket and dialled Chris' number.

It took an hour before Ash opened the door. Chris hadn't answered. It was an hour filled with dread and fear. *What had Chris set him up for? Why was the man so angry?* An official organisation would call the police if they thought there was an intruder. Warehouse workers don't just run around screaming trying to hurt people. He knew if he opened that door, he would be just the other side, ready to carry on his rage filled vendetta. His only hope was to get hold of Chris. Looking at his phone, he realised what the problem was. Inside a lorry, he didn't have any signal. *Could he wait until Chris returned? What if it took all night?* He strained trying to hear any sounds of the man. The shouting had stopped but he could occasionally hear something clunking in the background. Ash had pulled the strap on the shutters all the way down. There was a loop to secure it, and he stacked boxes on top of the strap. It would take a lot for the lunatic to open it, thinking about the size of him he added a few more boxes just in case.

A clinking sound alerted him as someone approached. He put his ear to the door as the sound got louder. Ash screamed as a blade went through the door. The maniac laughed, and rammed it back into the door, he was cutting a hole. Ash screamed again, and realised that the man was coming in no matter what Ash did. A feeling of rage swept through him. After everything that had happened to him, some lunatic with a knife wanted to kill him. Well, *not today* he thought. He pushed the boxes off the strap and threw the door up. With the door moving, he threw himself out of the lorry and at the madman. Thankfully, the knife clattered to the floor. The crazed man, taken by surprise with Ash leaping at him, fell to the ground, with Ash on top of him. Ash tried to punch him, and ended up pushing him in the face. He was too close. Managing to pull back and punch the man hard once in the face was all he could do before Ash was pinned with both arms and thrown into some boxes. Ash was dazed. His eyes blurred, and there was no doubt he was concussed. Feebly, he tried to rise. All he could see was the man walking towards him, knife in hand. He scrambled, moving quicker but it wasn't enough. The maniac was in front of him now. Ash looked up, and saw him let out a cry of laughter. The walking tattooed mountain that he was, was crying with laughter. He dropped the knife, and sat down wiping tears from his eyes. Ash took the opportunity to grab the knife, and rushed towards him but he was just thrown off again.

The man put his hands up, taking the blade Ash had dropped and

## The Girl Who Laughed At Birds

chucked the knife away, laughing. "You should have seen the look on your face. It was priceless. Wish I had a photo. Cheer up, Chris will be here in a minute."

Chris did arrive shortly, and it was best to say he wasn't happy. Ash had retreated to the other side of the warehouse, as soon as the lunatic had stopped his attack. The man, who had introduced himself as Vinny, had got to work in putting the boxes and the warehouse back together from their tussle. Ash had no interest in helping, or getting close to the man. Ash was just stemming the flow of blood from a cut on his elbow when Chris walked in. He took one look at Ash, his elbow and the aftermath of destruction left behind. "What the fuck happened here?" Chris demanded. He was staring at Ash, and looked like he might even hit him. "Erm, don't ask me. Sasquatch over there tried to turn me into a stab test dummy."

"What do you mean?" Ash's comment had been enough to divert Chris from what was obviously going to be a tirade on how bloody useless he was.
"Well, I had finished my packing, and he came in."

"Well you should have told him you had a good reason to be here."
"I did. I'm not stupid. Only he decided to turn into the hulk. I had to hide in the lorry. Which he then decided to put holes in."
"He what?" Chris' face had been turning gradually redder as the conversation continued. Ash didn't know what possible trouble the tiny little accountant could do to the man mountain but he hoped it would be a lot. That man was insane.

It only occurred to Ash as Chris went striding up and starting shouting at Vinny. How would Vinny take it that Ash grassed him up? It probably was not the best idea to anger the man, especially if he would have to work together at any point. Hopefully Chris could scare him enough that he wouldn't think about revenge. It did not seem likely though. *Great,* he thought, *I've made another friend.*

After a good half an hour, the hulking brute of a man walked over to Ash. Chris was following closely, and Ash could see that Vinny had been told in no uncertain terms that he was out of order. He reached out a hand to Ash as he approached, "I'm sorry, I got a little carried away. Won't happen again. Wanted to see if you'd run or panic at the first sign of danger. It turns out, when push comes to shove you don't just sit there and die. It's good to know about a man." Ash knew the man was being serious, but he couldn't quite believe that Chris associated with people this insane. At what point in a warehouse, would he need to fight danger? There was never going to be an occasion where an axe murderer walks in the door, or he would have to be in a gunfight. *It was a tiny town on the coast, not Iraq for god's sake.*

"Well, glad I proved myself I guess. Are all the tests done now?" The man nodded, "In that case, apology accepted. And I don't usually make it a point of ratting someone out immediately, but the whole stabbing a knife through the lorry door was an issue. Y'know?"

The man grinned, "I think fair is fair. Let's call it quits?"

"It should never have bloody happened. Do you remember what happened the last time you tried to surprise a newbie?" Chris interjected, "I should have had this conversation *before* I brought Ash in. But it's done now. You best hope that the lorry doesn't get pulled over or it will be coming out of your pay. Put some duct tape over it for the time being." Vinny scurried off, suitably chastised.

Ash turned to Chris asking, "So what did happen to the last newbie?"

Chris face darkened as he replied, "Vinny thought it would be funny to make him jump, see what he was made of. The problem was he was on a ladder cleaning the second story window, boy broke both legs and an arm. The man just doesn't think. Cost us loads to keep the boy quiet, especially when Vinny thought he would send him a Mr men card with Mr Bump on it."

"Why did you have to keep it quiet?"

"My clients like anonymity and peace of mind. That means no lawsuit and no police attention."

"What about me?"

"You're different. You're family and that loyalty will take us a long way. Just remember to keep your mouth shut, don't rock the boat and you will get paid well. You could pay for all the acting lessons you want, have all the money you need for university. No need for debt, or worries. You could be set up for life."

"Really? Even on £100 a day, I would need to work forever to get that much."

"No, I would sort you out. You just need to trust me. Give me three months, and you have to promise that whatever you hear, and whatever you see, you keep quiet about it. I know I can trust you, but your life might depend on it."

"Absolutely".

Ash would do it for the money. He could buy whatever he wanted then, have whatever house he wanted. It would be the dream.

It turned out Chris had only turned up to check in on the work Ash had done, and to pick up some items. He told Ash to move a whole load more boxes from one side of the room, closer to the loading bay for the next morning's load out. This time it was crates of beer and barrels of lager. He made a point of telling Ash that he couldn't get any beer out of the pressurised containers, you needed a pub system to do that and if he put a hole in the barrel the whole thing would be ruined. Ash eyed him and nodded, he didn't know whether the instruction was for him or Vinny, but it didn't matter. "When are you coming back?"

"I will meet you back at the house alright? You can grab a lift into town with Vinny when he drops the lorry off."

It took another two hours to move everything across the warehouse, and Ash was beyond tired. His arms ached, and his eye twitched from always keeping the tattooed man in his field of vision. No matter what either of them said, he did not want to be surprised again. He had even found a plank of timber and left it by the boxes. Ash wasn't angry with the man, he just didn't trust him. If he decided he did not like being shouted at by Chris, all he would have to do is lock the door and Ash would be at his mercy. They didn't talk at all for those two hours and Ash did not put his headphones back on.

## CHAPTER 23 – RENDEZVOUS

Eventually, it was time to shut up shop. Vinny waved at him to get in the lorry and started up the truck. As the truck got moving, Ash realised he could smell the man next to him. It was not an enjoyable experience. The stale odour of sweat quickly filled the car, so he opened the window. He realised the smell could also be him as well. The drive wasn't a long one, but he was rather surprised when they pulled into an empty car park near the harbour. There were two very grumpy men waiting for them. Ash assumed they were here for the two men as the car park was deserted apart from that.

Vinny turned the engine off and got out of the cab. Ash stayed where he was, wondering what was happening. He was sure that business hours weren't usually done this late. Nobody moved for a moment, and Vinny opened the door and shouted up to him. "Oi, idiot. Get out of the truck." Ash quickly shuffled out, blushing as he did so. He waved to the two men but got no reply as he greeted them.

"Is it all there?" The shorter of the two asked, he had a very heavy French accent. He didn't sound like he had a full grasp of English. "Yeah, all there," and with that Vinny walked off, grabbing Ash by the shoulder as he did so. Ash took the hint and walked off in the same direction. It was about two miles into town from where they were.

"They weren't very talkative, were they? Who do they work for?" Ash asked. Vinny gave him a funny look, and didn't say anything.

Ash thought that the men could at least have given them a lift in to the town. Why did they not just pick it up at the warehouse? It seemed a bit weird for Ash and Vinny to have to drop the lorry off and then have to walk back. Thankfully, it seemed Vinny did not plan on walking. There was another car at the far end of the car park.

The brute of a man had not spoken to Ash, apart from getting him out of the truck. Ash had become increasingly worried at the silence. Had the man really forgiven Ash for grassing him up? This new car was a ford Ka. It was a ridiculous size for Vinny. Ash snorted when he saw it and the man's face darkened. He quickly got in and then felt the suspension sink as Vinny got in the other side. The car tilted to the side. Vinny started it up and pulled out of the car park. Ash tried to push his body as far to the passenger side as possible, as his knee was in the way when Vinny wanted to change gear. He thought he might tell the man where to drop him off but decided against it. It was not the time to irritate him.

The radio came on and Ash was surprised to hear classical music coming out of it. He looked over at the brute, seeing a new perspective.
"Not the sort of thing I would pick for you. Any favourites?" Ash asked, trying to make conversation.
"Not the thing I would pick, it's the only station with signal. Can't lock into any of the others." They lapsed back into silence after that. Ash didn't attempt any more conversation and watched the world as they drove by. It had been a long day and he was tired. His arms barely worked, and his stress levels were at an all-time high. If and when he eventually arrived home, he would walk straight upstairs and pass out. Preferably for a day or two. His tiredness did not however, stop him from being on edge. There was a faint feeling of paranoia in his brain, and he couldn't help but feel like it was justified. He was being driven around by a man who had quite recently been waving a knife at him. In the end though, the tiredness won. If the man was going to kill him, at least he might get a good night's sleep. As the car stopped, he bumped his head against the window. He must have fallen asleep because as he woke up he heard himself grunt loudly in a suspiciously snore like way. Vinny laughed at him, and gestured for him to get out
"You're not used to a full day's work are you?"
"It's not that, the last few days have just been a bit of a rollercoaster."
"Well, either way, you best get yourself sorted out. And don't ask questions like you did earlier. It's fine with me, now I know you can

be trusted but the others... they won't stand for it. Keep quiet, nod and carry on. Anyway, see you tomorrow." Ash waved at him in acknowledgement and walked off back to Chris' house. *Great, I have to work with Mr Stabby some more,* he thought. He stumbled back home, up the steps to the flat and passed out promptly in his bedroom. He didn't even take the time to take his clothes off.

And that was how the week went for Ash constantly stacking lorries, signing off on any new deliveries and working with Vinny at all times. Ash preferred calling him Mr Stabby in his head but would never dare call him that out loud. After the first day, Vinny had been nice to Ash, but did not talk too much. Often they would go hours without speaking, unless they had to discuss what to do next. Chris had kept his word with paying Ash, and he now had more money than he ever had in one go. His uncle had told him to keep it stored at the house and not to bother putting it in the bank for the time being. He mumbled something about taxes and Ash realised how little he knew. He hadn't had a "real" job before, and he knew nothing about how to pay tax. *Did he have to go out of his way to pay it? Like, did he have to phone them?* He decided in the end to follow Chris' advice, and would get him to sort out the taxes. After all, he was an accountant.

Apart from the obvious, there were many reasons why Ash called Vinny "*Mr Stabby*". He didn't just have the one knife. When Ash showed up on the second day, the first thing he was shown was Vinny's collection. He had a blanket roll filled with knives. It turned out, he was an enthusiast. He had a meat cleaver with a massively thick blade, a filleting knife, multiple Stanley blades, a Swiss army knife, some commando knives (whatever that meant) and his showcase piece: the machete. Vinny's face lit up in delight as he discussed every knife, what they were used for and how he took care of them. Each one had a history, and he loved describing what they could do. The meat cleaver was apparently called a Chukabocho, and it was no standard blade of course. It was Damascus steel, Vinny was quick to point out. Everything that he owned had sharp edges, ornate handles and were perfectly balanced of course. When he came around to the machete, he held it as if it were a piece of god itself.

"This is a Parang machete, commonly called a Golok. It has a heavy weighted blade. This one is carbon-steel. It's beautiful. My pride and joy. British army use these things, and they use them well. This one has been with me through thick and thin." Looking at the knives with adoration, Vinny seemed like he was about to tear up. Ash assured him all his knives were beautiful and tried to steer him on to a different topic as quickly as possible. Putting the knives away took considerably longer than Ash assumed. Each knife was oiled and put back into its individual case. Every knife was put back in exactly the same order. There was a reason for their companiable silence, Vinny enjoyed it, and Ash was petrified.

Each day there was a different priority, and a different batch of things that needed shipping. Ash had not worked out what companies they worked with, or what specifically they dealt with but it seemed to be everything. It seemed they were a shipping company for anything that anyone needed. They had packed TVs, laptops, frozen meat, soft drinks and just about every other shipment of item he could think of. At the end of each day, they loaded up the lorry, each one a different make and took it to a location to be picked up. They always left in a car that was left for them to pick up, and Vinny dropped him off home. It did occur to Ash that something was unusual, when he realised on the third day that the keys were always in the car, and that it was a different vehicle every time. He made a joke about the KA not being good enough for Vinny, and again all he got was stares. It was a good week of work for Ash, he was tired enough each day that he went home and passed out. He had his music on his phone, and he managed to pretend for the most part, that there wasn't a maniac with knives just a few feet away from him at all times. Chris wasn't to be seen much, but everyday there was an envelope with money in it for him. He had made £400 so far this week and he didn't have much to spend it on. Every day he bought a lunch from a snack bar on the industrial estate and that was all he spent.

It was Friday, and Ash was ready for the weekend to start. They told him that after today he was done for the week. He hadn't thought much about anything for the past few days, he had just tried to focus on work and push everything out of his mind. The police had cleared him and now he just needed to get himself sorted out.

Maybe he could do some shopping at the weekend, buy some new clothes. He had never had this much money to just go out and spend before. Ash was looking forward to finishing at 5, and was just collecting his things, ready to go, when Vinny upset his plans. "Change of plan, we have another delivery coming, but something has gone wrong. We need to go and collect it from the harbour." Ash put his things back down and sighed. *Just think of the money he thought.*

It turned out that the delivery hadn't actually arrived yet. It would turn up at 10. Ash didn't have any way of getting back into the town, so had to wait with Vinny. As always, with any spare time, he had gone back to oiling his knives. Ash had come into work early during the week and had caught him practicing with them. It seemed he was not content with having them as only ornaments. He had a painted wooden target on a wall that he threw knives at, and had logs that he would practice his machete on. They were always put away when it was time to start work but Ash noticed he still carried one, a short blade in a sheath on his hip. It was a black knife, partially serrated. When Ash asked him, he said it was a SOG knife and his best friend. He didn't ask anymore, that was the knife he had used to cut open the door. He knew just how dangerous it could be.

---

## CHAPTER 24 - REALISATION

Ten o'clock arrived, and they made their way down to the harbour with the night darkening. Ash had started work that day early and his arms, legs and back ached. He had thought he might venture out into the nightlife tonight, but that was becoming more and more unlikely. The harbour was quite pretty at night. The edges of the town were set into a hill with the sea right at the bottom. The hill was a big one and there were two tiers of archways set into the stone, illuminated by light. Imagining for a second that he was a sailor in years gone by, sailing home to the lights of the harbour. The pier was one side of the wall that protected the boats, with a gap in the middle to comprise the harbour mouth. They drove down to the bottom of the hill, and then down past the second set of archways. Ignoring the tackle shops and workshops that had been built into the cliff face, they passed a security guard at a toll booth. He barely looked up from his magazine. Vinny flashed a wave and a smile at him, and then drove past. Obviously, Vinny was known around here.

They stopped at a boat moored low down in the water. Quickly and quietly, Vinny got out and waved to them. The two men on the boat acknowledged him with a nod but did not say anything. Ash hopped out and started picking up boxes, loading them into the van. This was the first time they had not used a lorry, and Ash had been surprised to see that it looked like a fairly new van. It was a transporter and had loads of space in the back. For some reason there were already a few boxes in there, which after the crates from the water had been loaded, were put at the back of the van. So they would be the first to be seen if anybody opened it. Ash put it down to Vinny's eccentricities.

As they had packed out the van, one of the boxes had spilt on Ash. He brushed off the white flour quickly so as not to make him dirty. Vinny looked at him, and said something to the men. It wasn't a pleasant conversation and Ash was happy to leave as quickly as they did. Vinny's hand moved to his waist as he talked. Everyone noticed that he was stroking his knife, and that cut any arguments short. Ash breathed easy as they got into the van without incident. This time when they went back to the warehouse, they unloaded the boxes immediately. They put them in the warehouse, in a separate storage area to the others. Vinny phoned multiple people, and he could be heard shouting across the warehouse down the phone. It seemed he was very unhappy about the box spilling. Ash asked how long it would be until they could go home, but Vinny just smiled at him whenever he asked. He often heard mutterings on "the staying power of youngsters" and how "kids don't know what hard work is", so after that he kept quiet.

"Right, we need to clean this van. Get the hose," Vinny said in a gruff voice. It was obvious he was still angry.

"Why do we need to do that? Because the flour got everywhere?" Vinny looked at him disbelieving, "Are you for real? Ok, whatever helps you sleep at night. Yes the flour got everywhere. Now clear it up quickly." He had put a weird emphasis on the word flour. *As if it was something else. What could it be?* Ash couldn't think of anything else that had the same consistency. They cleaned the van, only the inside. It was a deep clean, with not only fairy liquid, but bleach wherever any spillages were. Ash thought it was overkill, and didn't help lessen his sense of unease. He would have to ask Chris, whether he had been involved in anything dangerous. But he wouldn't do that to him surely? *But then come to think of it, why would he be asked to pick up flour late at night from a boat? He had not spent any time thinking of the things he had been doing. Why would you pick anything up late at night? Was it?... No it couldn't be... He had to think there was another solution. This wasn't a movie after all.* Anyway, one thing was for sure, he wasn't going to be asking Vinny. At least not if he was still stroking his knife.

His back was creaking, arms like lead as they finally finished cleaning the van. He had thought they were finished half an hour ago but Vinny had sent him back to scrub it down with a sponge while he unloaded some cases and packed them into two bags. He motioned Ash to him and hesitated a moment before he spoke. It looked like he was trying to work out what to tell him.

"Ok, so we have two bags. Usually, I wouldn't get somebody in their first week to do deliveries but that boat came at the wrong time. We need to move these bags. I am going to take one, and you're going to take one. Don't let anyone stop you, and do not for fucksake leave it anywhere. If you do, I will have to come looking for you, and it will come out of your wages. Are we clear?"

Ash nodded, not trusting himself to speak or look at the knife by Vinny's side.

"Ok so this is what I need you to do…"

Somewhere along the night, Ash realised that he was doing something illegal. It was not a new feeling considering the last few weeks. It didn't bother him as much as it should but he did not want to be a criminal. Ash didn't even know if he had the stomach or skills for it. Do people do apprenticeships for it? He chuckled at the image of a criminal CV then carried on walking, making sure not to speed up. Ash had told Vinny it wasn't part of his job description but the man was adamant that he was the right guy for the job. Ash, out of fear, threatened to tell Chris. Vinny had laughed. It was Chris' idea. Vinny's last words were, "Do you want a lawyer or not? You owe us."

If it was possible, he would have run away as soon as they departed and he had given that some consideration. It was perfectly possible to stash the bag in the warehouse, or a hedge or just set fire to it. As long as he wasn't connected to it he didn't care. The thought that kept him walking in a clearly fucked up situation was Vinny, that and imminent jail. He was clear in no uncertain terms that there would be consequences if this job went wrong. The only thing to do, was to keep walking.

What did bother him was the fact that if he got caught, with what he suspected was in the package, he would be going to prison for as long as some serial killers. There was not much that he could do. He already had a bag full of suspicious substances, and if it was left anywhere, he would be to blame. He couldn't run away, and Chris had offered him some serious money if he stayed with him for a few months. At least now he knew what that money would be for. Chris and he were going to have words. The place he was going had been described to him in detail, and the man he was to meet. There were no names, no fancy passcodes. Just turn up, say "there's your stuff, apologies for the disruption" and leave quickly. It was a dusty pub, not far away from where they had taken the delivery from the boat. It was closer to the west than the east, but still not too far. Most of the town was in between the two hills on either side. The beach itself went for miles but really only the promenade and main beach by the pier was used by anyone. There were pubs and bars all along the sea front. The town centre itself was a circle, a literal centre with four paved pedestrian streets. One went to the harbour and was only a 2 minute walk to the sea, one went toward the east cliff, turning into a steep hill, one went west, the only bit of flat ground, and one went straight uphill, either north or south, Ash didn't really know which direction it was, apart from opposite to the harbour.

He had a black duffel bag. *Really inconspicuous he thought.* The package, whatever it was, was not heavy. It weighed less than a bag of sugar. He did not need a gym bag to carry it, and suggested a nice colourful rucksack next time to Vinny. It didn't go down well. It occurred to Ash that if you wanted to not look suspicious, a bag with superheroes on it, or something that didn't look like he was doing exactly what he was doing might be better. When he arrived at the town centre he walked west on a flat bit of road called King Street, past a Boots, Mcdonald's and pubs. Lots of pubs. They had live music on and looked like they were having a good time. It was 11 o'clock and everybody seemed like they were in high spirits. *So much for no witnesses.* The pub he arrived at looked like it hadn't been cleaned in years. There weren't many people in there, and those that were, were drunkenly slurring their words. Arguing about nothing in particular. Ash caught the words "bluey" and "eighth". He had no idea what they were on about. He walked up to the bar and sat on a stool. No one else was at the bar. He put the bag down and put his arms on the bar, waiting for the barman to turn around. He immediately regretted it as he realised the bar runner was wet. He lifted his arms and wiped off the stale alcohol. The man turned round, an old man with tattoos that had long sagged with age. He had an anchor on one arm and a skulls head on the other. He spoke in a quick drawl and it took Ash a good few second to work out what he had said. He had a thick Irish accent. "You're in the wrong place kid, what do you want?"

## The Girl Who Laughed At Birds

"Doubt it, a pint and I need to talk to Danny".

"Danny eh? Well your funeral. Pint o' what?"

Danny it turned out was a man in his mid-thirties. He walked with a swagger, and in all honesty was not someone Ash would voluntarily talk to. He looked well… rough.

"Who the fuck are you?" Danny spoke, getting in his face and looking him right in the eye. Breath stinking of booze, he had a weird energy about him. It was a real possibility that he could be stabbed in this bar and nobody would notice. His palms shook, and he could feel sweat starting to drip off his forehead and onto the bar. "I have your stuff, apologies for the disruption." Ash got up to leave, forgetting the pint in front of him. The man grabbed his arm. "Oh no you don't. What happened?"

"I don't know, I just know there was an issue. I got told to say sorry, and give you your stuff," Ash's voiced had gone up an octave or two.

"Why do you keep saying stuff? Are you a narc?" The bar had stopped chatting now and all turned to look at him.

Ash winced as the pressure on his arm increased, "No, I don't know what's in the bag. I'm just a middle man. Can I go now?"

"Well maybe we should get you to try some eh?" There was laughter all around and Ash choked out some more apologies. The man grunted.

"Go on, fuck off. Tell 'em that next time I want a discount. They told me they wouldn't fuck up."

Ash walked out as quickly as he could. He tried to not break out into a run but he sped up as he got to the door.

He slowed when he got back to the middle of the town. He looked back and was sure after a few minutes that the man was not following him. Chris' flat was north about 15 minutes' walk away. He was too angry to see him. They had blackmailed him. It wasn't as if he could run away home. Bastards.

Nat was right, Chris was dodgy. Nat had said that it was suspect, he magically had a lawyer who was fine with him committing crimes. Ash was very tempted to go and put a brick through his car window out of spite. So going home was out of the question and Nat very well might be out to kill him. He sped up again, feeling an icy chill. He tried to look around in all directions but he couldn't do it.

Where was safe? Steven didn't want to know him anymore. Not after all the police involvement. His stomach rumbled loudly as he realised he was starving. He hadn't eaten since lunch, and it was almost midnight.

Walking down to the harbour the only places open were kebab shops, filled with drunks. He didn't need that right now, but he knew that there were fish and chip shops which stayed open for the die-hard fishermen. They didn't close until around 2 o'clock. At least it would be warm.

## CHAPTER 25 - DECISIONS

He bought a cod and chips. It was the first thing he could see, and he just wanted some food. He passed the woman in the shop some money, picked up a plastic fork and walked out. Stuffing his mouth with food, which was decidedly too hot for him, Ash sat down on a bench. There was no point trying to stuff his face and walk. It had been a long day, Ash looked down and realised that he still didn't fully have all the powder wiped off his clothes. If that wasn't a dead giveaway, nothing was. He brushed it off with his sleeve, careful not to get any on his hands. He didn't want to mix it with his chips, he doubted he would sleep for days if that happened.

It had been a strange week for Ash. Getting arrested, then charges being dropped, then potentially committing an even worse crime. There were a lot of problems on his list. He could row with Chris when he got back, and make it clear that he wanted nothing to do with any of the deliveries. He choked as he realised why Chris has called him a courier. Ash might as well be called "the mule" from now on, but all of that could be dealt with. Negotiating with family was possible, but with Nat, he wasn't so sure.

He had his life back, yet he knew something was wrong with what happened. Nat went out the same night the guy was murdered. It must have been Nat. How did they not realise that? More to the point, what was she going to do to him? He had ratted her out, and they must have told her. He doubted she would just let that go. After the first text she sent, he had replied once and then ignored her. She had sent a few more, but he had no plans in being caught alone with her. If she wanted revenge she was perfectly capable of it. She might even get a kick out of it. I mean how many people did she have to kill to be a serial killer? He thought he had heard it had to be a minimum of 3 somewhere, he did not want to be the one that made up the quota.

He wolfed down his fish and chips as quickly as he could. He wanted to finish up and get home as quickly as possible. Hopefully, he would sleep all morning tomorrow. Now, was there a bin anywhere? He looked around for one and that's when he saw him.

The haggard man looked even worse than he did before. He obviously wasn't washing often, and was sleeping rough. The man looked up and gave a start as he saw Ash.

"So you're back are you. Are you here to kill me off?"

*Fucksake*, Ash thought. *I do not need this.* "Mate, I'm just getting rid of my chips and I'm gone. How am I meant to know which bench you sleep on each night? Have a good one." And with that he walked off.

The man called out in a soft voice, "So did the boy die? Bet he did." Ash paused. He really did not want to talk to this nutjob, but well… he was right. "Yes, he died," he said softly.

"And am I right in saying, in suspicious circumstances?"

"Her.. Heroin overdose," Ash stuttered.

"Oh, and does that usually happen to coma patients?" Ash remained silent. It was obvious to both of them, that it was not natural causes. It was clear what had happened. "Do the police have her?"

"They let her go."

The tramp punched the wall in frustration. He shouted, and he raged, "She's done it again. She's gotten away with it."

"Yes. Yes she has," Ash whispered.

He gazed out to the sea in the cold night air. *What possessed her to do these things? Did she get a kick out of them?*

"She leaves a wreck wherever she goes. Look what damage she has done to you. The grief you have been given. She made you do things didn't she? She dragged you into her world, and corrupted you. Just like my son. Do you think she knows the damage she causes? I'm certain in fact, that she does. She likes it. She will sacrifice anyone. As long as she survives."

"It wasn't all like that you know. Things just happened."

"They always do, and they always will. Tell me honestly, do you think this is the end? Do you think that if we both walk away now, everything will stop? That there will be no more damage, no more lives ruined?"

Ash was silent. He couldn't guarantee that. He knew that this would carry on. Not only that, there was a feeling of guilt gnawing at him. She had gotten away with it. She deserved prison for what she did. Killing a man in cold blood was not something that could be forgiven. How did she live with herself?

"I see, so the question is. What do we do now?"

"We?" Ash asked surprised.

"Yes, as long as she is free, people are going to get hurt. They are getting hurt. How can you let this go?"

Ash hesitated. He had to deal with Nat in some way, if not then he might be next. "What do you suggest?"

"The police can't touch her. We need to get rid of her." Ash backed away from the man as he talked so casually of killing someone. Tonight had shown him that he was not prepared for a twenty year stretch. "Well. Isn't it obvious? We get her to own up to it. She needs to face justice, she needs to be sent to prison for what she did." Ash was sure this man would do anything to stop her, recording her was the best option, and least drastic. "And how do you think that is going to work? If you can get her to do that which I highly doubt, then what stops her blaming it all on you?"

"I will record it, I will get her confessing out of her own mouth. That will do it." Ash was sure now. This was the answer. He could meet up with her, get her to admit it and then send it to the police. "And what if she incriminates you, what she made you do. What will you do then?"

"I will have to accept my fate, as long as we get her, that's all that matters."

## CHAPTER 26 - CONFRONTATION

Ash did in fact sleep until noon. When he finally awoke, he immediately texted Nat.

Ash: *I can meet today, how about coffee?*
Nat: *I thought you might want to come round mine?*
Ash: *Maybe it's best to be in a place where you can't throw glasses at me. That good?*
Nat: *Coffee shops have glasses idiot... sure thing.*

His mind had not changed. Something had to be done. Two people had died, and multiple families were hurt. The police obviously didn't know what they were doing, and he had a solution. If he could make sure that this didn't happen again, then he had an obligation. In the back of his mind he knew, he would be next on the list. The fact that he knew everything, and had given her up must have angered her. She would be coming for him next. He had to make sure he did this today, and that she didn't get a chance to kill him. Nat couldn't get to him in public, there he was safe.

He arrived early at the coffee shop, making sure he knew where the exits were this time. Grabbing a coffee, he put his phone on record in his pocket. The table was far away from others so they could talk without being overhead. Within minutes, Nat arrived. She was still beautiful, whatever her faults. Draping her coat over her chair, she readjusted as she sat down. He could see the lines of her collarbone as she leant forward to take a sip. Ash deliberately did not look down her top. It was time to focus, she had killed people. She was a bad person. Nat only used her looks to get people to do what she wanted. He could not fall for that trap. Her face lit up as she saw him.

"So here we are, two free people. Doesn't the air taste sweeter?" She asked, moving to sit on the other side of the small table; rather worryingly within arms-reach. He could smell her perfume now, the smell of roses permeating the air.

"Well, I knew I hadn't done anything wrong. I had faith that they knew what they were doing and would let me go," Nat's smiled dropped as she notices Ash's tone of voice.

"God, I forgot how naïve you were. Nothing wrong? Don't give me that. You were the one who hurt him. You did all the damage to him. If anything, you're more to blame than I am. All I did was walk home and get attacked," She smiled sweetly at him, to drive the point home.

"Funny, I wasn't the one who left home for a long time on the night he died."

"Oh yeah, and I have load of heroin stashed in my bag in case of emergencies." Her eyebrow arched, almost daring him to say it. To accuse her. The silence stretched.

"Well, do you?" She laughed at that, a full throated laugh. Drawing looks from others, she carried on for a full minute. "That's not an answer. Tell me, did you do it?"

"I could kiss the person that did. They saved our asses. Whoever did that is our guardian freakin' angel. I even thought for a moment…"

"What?" Ash asked.

"Well, all the time I was out of the house, no one knew where you were. We only have your word to say that you were at my place. I thought maybe you did it. You know for love?"

"For love? What do you mean?"

"Well, an innocent young boy like you. Infatuated, wanting to get attention. Wanting to stay over… I thought maybe you did it to get my attention. To get in my bed," She laughed softly, "Then I remembered how much of a pussy you are. You could never have done it."

Ash didn't believe her. It all just seemed so convenient. There must be a way to get her to open up.

"I thought about it y'know. Matt said it would be best for everyone if he didn't wake up. I thought about it but realised, that's not me. I couldn't do it. I didn't have it in me. Whoever did that, saved us. I want to thank them, so I thank you."

"You really think I did it, don't you? You little rat. I know you told the police I wasn't at home. Wait…" She looked around him, then lunged for him and grabbed his top. She looked down his chest and then even pulled up his top. Ash stumbled back off his chair. "I thought for a second you were wearing a wire." "What is this, CSI? They used big ass wires in the 70s, not now." Nat's eyes narrowed.

"Show me your phone."

"No," he said, moving away from her grip.

"Show it to me" she demanded.

"You can't make me."

She grabbed his shirt and pulled him close. Speaking clearly for any microphone to be picked up.

"I did not kill him, I did nothing wrong. He was a sadist and a sicko, and I want to send flowers to whoever killed him. But. It. Was. Not. Me. Got it?"

She stormed out.

## CHAPTER 27 - MISTAKES

The door banged shut, courtesy of Nat's dramatic exit. It was not his finest hour. Hands trembling, he wiped the sweat of his face. The waitress asked him if he was ok, like there was an answer to that. *"No, I'm about to be murdered"* would not go down well. He would not put it past her to be hiding behind a lamppost. *Couldn't she see what she had done?* More and more he realised that she would just continue being her. One thing was for sure if she wasn't trying to kill him before, she would be now.

The walk home was bitterly cold. The breeze had picked up and the rain had begun to fall. His neck was hurting from looking from side to side, and his eyes twitched. The main thought that kept on spinning through his brain, was *run away*. This whole trip out to his uncle's had become a serious clusterfuck. He was meant to recharge, get a job and have a life. Instead, someone died and he was in the middle of it between a murderer and life in prison. Not only that, but the killer he had repeatedly betrayed . It was not ideal, in fact it was a horrific situation to be in. He felt like he was in a horror film, in the woods, in a locked house waiting to see where the killer would pop out from. It was shredding his nerves.

Adding to his growing sense of paranoia was the fact that he knew he could not run away. It was a glorious idea when he first thought of it. He even started packing his bags. He had enough money to travel home, or he could even get a train and stay in a town like Folkestone and nobody would find him. He could be free. The only issue with that, is that he was now hip deep in work for Chris. There had been no more package drop offs since he had returned to work, they had relegated him back to warehouse duty once he had passed on his message; but he was now "involved".

He had returned from that night out, nerves shredded, wide awake to see Chris waiting up for him. Ash gave him every expletive he could fling at him.

"What the fuck was that? I'm not a fucking gangster... whatever the fuck you do, I don't want a piece of it," Chris grabbed him, hand over his mouth.

"Shout all you fucking want at me," he hissed, "But don't you dare say a word about what happened. Do you want the world to know? I have neighbours and walls have fucking ears." Ash tried to wriggle out and Chris eventually let him. Ash took a swing at him and Chris put him in a headlock. Grunting and cursing Ash strained against his uncle but for all of his diminutive size he couldn't budge him.

Chris let go and backed away, "Look I'm sorry. In my business, we help each other out. I do the accounts for many businesses, making sure they all can get their money to where they can use it. Sometimes it's not all legal, but that's what I do. I make sure that money flows, and nothing looks out of place. Now because I am trusted, they also ask me to store things, like extra goods they don't want to declare etc. Recently, they have had a distribution problem and have asked me to fix it. I have, but it is not something I want to be doing. It is not something I would have involved you with, and I will make sure it doesn't happen again. But you want more money than you can spend? Listen and learn. And do not go shouting about our fucking business where people can hear. When you work with these people, they look after you if you keep your nose clean." And with that he went back to his room.

Ash understood the principle, but did not agree at all. He did not want to be involved in anything like this. It was basically very illegal, and not something he would have let himself do, if he had known. Instead, he had ended up being an accidental drugs trafficker. *Brilliant.* That night had simultaneously set his brain fixed on the idea that he should get as far away as he could, whilst also making him feel trapped. How could he leave? His uncle had essentially confessed to crimes, Ash had committed crimes however much he did not mean to. If he suddenly dropped and left, they would worry that he was going to snitch. *Let's face it,* he thought, *I have got a track record.* There was no real way out. He couldn't ask Chris to let him go, who knows what he might do. So he went back to the warehouse, pretending all was normal, whilst twitching continuously trying to work out where Nat might spring from to get her revenge.

It came to him whilst washing dishes of all things. He needed a solution to at least one of his problems. He had to either sort out Nat, and the fallout that was bound to be coming; or to extricate himself from Chris' criminal enterprise. He couldn't do both, at least not immediately. So he had worked out, that he needed to choose one to do first. It came down to simple mathematics in the end. Who would be more trouble? What problem would be more complicated to deal with? Nat was one person. There were no other complications, and put simply: he was in more immediate danger with her. She would be actively trying to find ways to hurt him, ways to get him alone and kill him.

He finished the dishes and set about solving the problem of Nat. He had tried incriminating her and it had not worked. It had made her suspicious of him, and he was sure now she would be expecting something. She knew where he lived, so it did not make sense to just stay here until she snuck through in the middle of the night. *He would never sleep again.* The only way he would get through this alive, was to be proactive; he had to get her, before she came back on a murderous rampage. She must have connections, how did she even get heroin in the first place?

It needed to be in the next few days. Give her a week, and he knew he would be dead or permanently silenced somehow. He could ask Chris for help, but he did not think that was such a good idea. It felt like the fewer favours he asked for, the better he would be in the long run. No, he would not use Chris. He had to do this alone. Or did he? The tramp was always there, whatever he did to Nat, he could blame it on him. That man hated Nat, it was his only obsession. It had essentially ruined his whole life by coming here. Just sleeping on benches, waiting for an opportunity.

Ash was surprised he hadn't already gone to her house and confronted her. Why hadn't he? Ash would have to ask him. The more he thought about it, it became clearer. If he set up a meeting, Nat would suspect him. She would not think anyone else would be there. Nat wouldn't think that he would be dangerous. She thought of him as a little boy, like a bug to crush. That was good, it was better to be underestimated than overestimated. He would set up the meeting, and the problem would be solved. It occurred to him, that some would feel guilty in his place, but he found that he didn't. It was Nat or him. His life was on a countdown, and Nat might be coming for him at any moment because she was a killer. She was the real reason for all of this, and she was getting what she deserved. This wouldn't be a bad thing he was doing, this would be justice. For him, for Jax, and for the boyfriend that overdosed. He would have to ask the tramp what the kid's name was.

## CHAPTER 28 – PROBLEMS

Ash arrived at the beach. He had put on his best clothes, he didn't know why, but it felt right. He was surprised when Nat had agreed to meet him. He had thought he would have to do some begging, pleading and apologising. She usually liked to toy with him, but that was not the case this time. She agreed and asked him the time and place. Nat didn't even question why it was 10 o'clock on the pier. As if it was the most normal thing in the world. Another time Ash would have worried about that, but it didn't matter what she did now. There was a plan and the tramp was in on it. It would end tonight. There would be one less killer in the world. It was for the best.

Ash arrived early, it wouldn't do to be late on a night like tonight. It was important that she not see them both arrive, or talking to each other. She would know something was wrong then. He sat down at the furthest end of the pier. There was not a soul in sight. Ash was there, he knew where the tramp would be hiding. It hadn't taken much to convince him. Ash explained that they needed to get her off the streets as quickly as possible and she was too good at working him out. She was aware now of what he was trying to do. They had to work out a different solution. They would have to ensure that she didn't kill again. That left two options, get her to attack somebody else with witnesses, or the alternative. Ash would have preferred not to have to be so confrontational but he could see no other way. Ash had set up the meeting to talk to her. From there, they would see what option she would take.

The wind brought an icy chill with it, and whipped his coat around his face. It wasn't raining but he could feel the spray of the sea across his face. The sea raged around him. It looked like it might storm at some point. Ash hoped that it would hold for the time being. He was frozen to the bone after twenty minutes. He doubted he could have protected himself at that point, for fear of snapping himself in two; or that he would want to. Anything would be a mercy from this cold.

The winds battered the pier, the surf tried its best to crash over the top, to dominate the wall. Each time it failed, but it got closer. Ash was mesmerised by the constant barrage of water. It was so persistent. He felt insignificant, tiny, when faced with the vastness of the ocean in front of him. If he fell, no one would know. The way the sea was today, he would drop in and be dragged off in seconds. It would swamp him, and that would be it. He shivered, pulling his gaze from the torrent of water. She would be here soon and he had to be ready. Ash had once hoped that she would like him. In fact, a part of him still did. She was captivating. Not because of her beauty, that was a given, it was how uncompromising she was. How... confrontational. Everything she did, she did with all of her heart. It had occurred to him that if that were true, she also killed with all of her heart. That was something he could not forgive. People's lives were at risk, his life was at risk. In that same relentless way, she would silence him. Only he knew, the state she had come back the night of the murder. She didn't want to go to prison, she wouldn't be captured and subdued. No, she would come for him. It wasn't only self-preservation that fuelled him though. At least that's what he told himself. If he didn't do this, who was next? Ash's life had been put on hold indefinitely, Jack Hawkins had died for her rage, she had killed her own boyfriend. No one had stopped her, and if he stepped aside, no one would until more people died. More grieving mothers and fathers, waiting for their son to come home. He would do this, so that no one else felt that pain. The consequences, whatever they were, would be met, as long as she did not continue doing what she did.

Nat appeared in the gloom. He could hear her shoes, assertively clicking along the stone pier. As always, she didn't hesitate or stop. She had agreed to meet him, and so she did. Her jacket was blowing in the wind below her waist, though she seemed altogether unaffected. Unlike Ash, who was trying desperately to stop his teeth chattering. Nat didn't slow, even though she didn't see Ash. She continued all the way to the end of the peer, apparently expecting him to be there. As she came closer, Ash waved and tried a friendly smile. It looked more like a grimace, so he stopped quickly.

Nat stopped a short distance away from him, looking him up and down.

"So, to what do I owe the pleasure? Came out for a little night time stroll?"

"I needed somewhere we could talk. Alone."

"No recording devices this time?"

"No, hand on my heart. Here," Ash chucked his phone at her. She caught it, turned it off and then threw it back at him.

"Ok, you've dragged me to the ass end of nowhere. Now's the time to talk, if not I'm going back in the warm."

Ash paused. He had thought of many different scenarios, what he would say to her. She would be angry, she might cry, but in the end she would admit the truth. He had to find the right words. "You say you didn't kill him?"

"Of course, I didn't. Killing people is a little bit far don't you think? We're not all cutthroats and murderers. This isn't the mafia. You don't just fucking off people. Is this what this is? You trying to… what? Get me to confess? You are a sad sack of shit. Go and live your life Ash. I couldn't deal with knowing my life is so desperately sad, like you do." She turned to leave, and then turned back, " You know, I actually thought you might be OK. You might be the one person I've met who doesn't think I'm evil, who actually has my back. Yeah you were a bit creepy, but well intentioned. Where has that person gone eh? Bit cloak and dagger this isn't it? Go and crawl back in your hole Ash. You disgust me," She threw her hands up, pulling her coat tighter, and started to walk down the pier.

Ash stepped closer a few steps and shouted. "You had a boyfriend. What happened to him?"

She rounded on him, "What the fuck did you just say?"

"You… you had a boyfriend. Back in London. What happened to him?" Ash asked.

There was silence for a while. Ash stared at her, arms in his pockets, waiting. It was Nat's turn now to stutter. "Who told you that? What did they say?"

"I want to hear it from you."

"Yes. I had a boyfriend."
"What was his name?"
"Dean."
"And what happened to him?"
"None of your fucking business."
"I think it is. He died, didn't he?"
"Don't you fucking dare," Nat rushed at him, arms raised at him in fury. Ash skipped back a few steps but he was ready for this. He would not back down from this.
"He died, of a heroin overdose. Pretty damn familiar if you ask me."
"You don't get to talk about him like that," Nat was shouting now, he could hear her clearly over the wind, "You don't get to tell me what's familiar and what's not."
"Well from where I'm standing, you've killed a lot of people."

Nat turned to leave, stopped and spoke, "You know what, I will tell you. We had everything, we had the fucking life and it all ended because he wanted more. The parties weren't enough, I wasn't enough. You have not woken up in the morning to find your lover dead. You haven't cried your heart out waiting for someone to wake up, knowing that they won't. You didn't see the whites of his eyes and you sure as hell don't see his dead face every morning and every time you sleep. So don't you damn well talk to me about him," Nat's breath was ragged. Her hair had fallen out and was whipping in the wind. She stared defiantly at him, daring him to talk more. Ash spoke softly, but she could still hear him, "Why did you do it? Did you mean to kill him? Either of them? I get Jack I guess, he would have sent you to prison forever. It was a big "Fuck you" to him. But your own boyfriend. Your lover. Dean was it? Did you plan it?"

"Did you not listen to a word I said? *He* wanted it, *he* was the party animal. *He* got into it by himself. I did nothing but stand by his side. I pulled him out of the gutter when he didn't make it home, I gave him money for the rent. I loved that man, so very much. He was straightening out. Dean was coming out of it for me. He said I saved him, and then he had one fucking relapse and he was dead. That was it. No more fucking Dean. No more life for me."
"Liar!" The tramp shouted as he ran into Nat. He hit his shoulder

against her, knocking her against the wall. He grabbed her by the hair, punching her in the face repeatedly. "You liar," he shouted again, "You killed him. You did it, you killed them all." He had kept punching her, and as Ash stood helpless, she went limp. The tramp in his rage threw her body against the wall and over the top. "What did you do?" Ash screamed at the man, pulling him closer by his collar, "What did you do? We weren't meant to fucking kill her." The tramps eyes were wide, his matted hair flying in the wind. "You saw her. She would deny anything. She is too clever. Better off dead," he turned away and walked back towards the town.

Ash looked over the wall but he couldn't see anything. He frantically searched up and down the harbour wall but saw no sign of her. It wasn't meant to go this way. Nat was going to give herself up, or attack him and get caught by the tramp filming. He had a speech planned, she was going to admit it all. He fell to his knees, rocking in the icy wind. Tears mingling with the rain that had started falling. The storm had broken, Nat had died, Ash had nothing. They had killed a killer, but all he felt was emptiness.

## CHAPTER 29 - CONSEQUENCES

Despair was not new to him. It was an old friend that popped up every now and then to remind him, that despite his best efforts, he had fucked up again. It hit him with waves of nausea and stole his breath. It hurt, and it did not stop. He had made it back to the flat, and once inside, his heart, body and brain gave out on him. His feelings for Nat were complex at best, but she should not have been drowned by some scumbag. It occurred to him that she might have survived, but he doubted it. She had been hit repeatedly and then thrown off the edge. It was a good 15 feet drop, and it might have been even bigger with a low tide. The coastguard would likely be scrapping her body off the rocks; that is, if the fish didn't get to her first.

At the thought of fish carving away at her face, he ran to be sick. The vomiting continued until he had nothing left. He wretched on repeat until he choked, tears streaming down his face. If the police came storming in this time, he would tell them everything. If anyone came in at that point he would throw himself at their mercy. The tramp had disappeared quickly with grim amusement; his work finally done. He would go back to society happy in the knowledge that a killer had been dealt with. Ash was not sure that by doing what they did, they were not worse themselves. The number of killers in the world had not diminished, because by ridding the world of Nat, two more people added their names to the list. Ash had not committed the act but he had been a participant. By law and in truth, he had been an accomplice. He had set the meeting and arranged for it all to happen.

Initially he had felt a glum satisfaction, but that had faded quickly. Had they performed justice? Had they been in the right? He had been so sure that Nat had been a killer. She had met his eyes and faced them both. She had not been lying. Nat had been at her most brutally honest, at her most vulnerable and Ash had betrayed her again. Her words echoed back to him "Did you not listen to a word I said?". Every time Ash had asked her questions, she had denied knowing anything; sometimes with a smile, sometimes with anger but always she denied it. She had kept to her story with the police, with Ash. And Ash was still a free man. No matter what had happened, he had not been betrayed.

The tramp, whatever his name was, had seemed unhinged. He was only there for revenge, and that was what had happened. No calmly asking for the truth, no ultimatum about opening up to the police. The plan had not been followed and Nat had not really had the opportunity to incriminate herself. Or protect herself at that. It dawned on him at the moment, that was no fair trial. It was an execution, and it was always intended to be one. He had helped someone he didn't know or like, kill someone. Kill a friend of his, while he did nothing to stop it. He went back to retching.

Hours later, Chris had returned to find Ash still in his cycle of despair, self-hate and self-justification. Chris took off his coat as he found him huddled over the basin. He sighed and sat down on the bath.

"This is becoming a habit, I'm not your nurse. You have to grow a backbone at some point boy," said Chris. His words were harsh but his tone was soft, gentle almost.

"What new calamity has happened this time? Had another lover's tussle? Chipped a nail?"

Ash snorted at that but spoke in halting breaths, "How do you live with this? How do you stand the guilt? The stress?" "Ah, that age old question. Most of us with a conscience, simply don't. It's not gangsters, the criminals or the police that will get us in the end. It's our own bloody guilt. What would you have me do? Waste away in this shithole? Sit on the side lines, begging for scraps while those who have the stomach for it, live the life we should all have?" He looked at Ash seeing his sunken eyes, his ragged breaths still struggling for air, "You will find money makes you sleep easier at night. It means I can do things like protect you, wave a hand and magically sort out things that could be life ending." It seemed to Ash that what Chris was saying had a hidden meaning but he simply didn't have the brain for it.

"Well you can't save me from myself it seems. I fucked up. I hurt someone," choked Ash.

"I know you did. You have had a busy few months, and it has gone a bit to shit hasn't it? It's done now though. He can't get you. He died from a heroin overdose that was nothing to do with you or Nat. So you're free and clear?"

Ash pulled himself up from the basin and turned to stare at his uncle.

"How do you know it wasn't Nat?"

"What do you mean? The police cleared her didn't they?"

"Yeah, but that could have been a technicality."

"It wasn't. I thought you would have realised. We have friends in high places. How the hell was she going to get into a hospital, inject a man with heroin and get out without getting caught? She's not a criminal mastermind. She doesn't have the resources, and I doubt very much she would go through with a thing like that. She would have been spotted picking up heroin for a start, I mean where is she going to find that in a town like this? Use your bloody brain Ash. It's done. You need to live the life you have, not the one you want. Now I have used up an almighty amount of favours for you. You're in with the big boys now. Do not fuck it up. I don't care what you do to get yourself sorted but do it quick. I want you back at work by tomorrow." And with that Matt left, not just the room but the apartment. He probably had some important meeting to go to. Ash knew now what meetings like that meant. They could mean that they were deciding which life to snuff out next.

It was clear now, as Ash cried and cried. He had never truly understood what was going on. The only person that was truly innocent was Nat. And she was now gone. That was on him; her life snatched away because he simply had not believed her. He hadn't believed the police, and it had never occurred to him to ask Matt. He snorted as the conversation came to him, would he have ever have asked, "err…. Sorry to ask, but did you assassinate a guy to make my life easier?" His life had gone far beyond just being wrong. He looked back at the last few months; since he had arrived, he had done one good thing, and many, many terrible things. She did not deserve what had happened. She never had.

It took time, but he crawled to the door of the bathroom and hauled himself up by the frame. His clothes were wet through and he decided to change them. He laughed at the suit laid out on the bed and thought *fuck it, why not?* Buttoning up the freshly pressed suit, he smiled for the first time in a long time. Tears still rolled slowly down his face, but he was ready. He switched off the light, leaving the keys to the flat on the kitchen side. He wouldn't be back.


The walk was not a long one. It took him across the town, the high street and it's only church. Nobody stirred, as if somehow being close to Ash would contaminate them all. In his life, he had often wondered how things would turn out. When would he have his first big acting break? When would he have his first serious girlfriend? The dreams of being on stage and staring out to an adoring crowd. He had dreamt of these every night for his entire teenage years. He loved to be adored, and he knew if he had his chance people would adore him. If only someone would give him a break. That adoration was lost for him now. He would be a footnote in the papers, an asterisk in the school year book. He would be a tale for others to follow, but a warning not an inspiration. Somewhere along the line he could have stopped this. It quite simply was not about him anymore. His actions had caused a life to end. Multiple lives in fact, but Nat's was the important one. That one was so incredibly clear to him. His life was over now, but he could tell the world, show them what had happened to Nat. They would not believe him, not to start off with. But the first thing they would do is look for her. She needed to be found, to have a loving family have the peace and closure that comes with knowing what happened in the final moments.

His life would be forfeit, and so it should. His life would end clean though, and the world would know what happened to Natalie.

## CHAPTER 30 – HONESTY

"So let's start from the beginning shall we?"

The policeman was the same acerbic man who had found Ash at the café. It was the same gruff face, indicating very clearly that he believed whatever Ash was going to say, it was going to be rubbish. With that face full of scepticism staring at him, Ash felt the first pangs of relief. He had made his decision, and it was the right one. It was not possible to make up for what had been done but he could try.

"I, of my own mind and free will, have decided to forego the option of a lawyer. I have come here under my own volition and not under duress. I was complicit in the murder of Natalie Carson. Here is what happened."

The interview went on for hours; there were no breaks but once the questions started coming the policeman ordered somebody to get some coffee. His scepticism faded, as he realised the truth of Ash's words. After Ash was reaching the part about him arranging a meeting with Nat and the tramp, the policeman stopped proceedings to ask him, "Now I must ask this, you're giving a lot of incriminating evidence. You have been an accessory to a murder, and you will be charged as such. Do you know what you are doing? Are you of sound mind enough to be doing this?"

Ash smiled. It was one of pain, with his eyes brimming with tears not yet released, "Once you've done something like this, you have to stand up to it. You have to face it, don't you officer? The damage is done, and all I can do now is tell the world how it went wrong. It won't absolve me, but at least her family will know what happened. She deserved better."

"Touching Ash, for the person who killed her."

Ash smashed his hand into the table. He fell backwards and rolled up to his feet with some slowness. Two police officers rushed in to restrain him, they reset the table, returned Ash to his seat and handcuffed him this time. Ash's chest heaved as he struggled for breathe, "I did not kill her, that part was not me."

"Sit down, you might as well have killed her. You arranged it, you made it happen and you betrayed her. Now who is this tramp you have been banging on about? Is he an alter ego of yours?"
"He's real, he sleeps down by the sea front."

"Ok, now we are going to stop this discussion here. We will make enquiries into what you have said. If what you have said is true, then you will be charged. You will be here until we can be sure of what has happened."

They led him in cuffs to the cell. Once inside, they undid his restraints, leaving him alone. He sat down on the bench, head in hands. All he had to do was wait until they found Nat's body. It should not take long, it was just on the side of the pier. He was surprised that somebody hadn't seen her fall in, or a fisherman had not accidentally caught her with a hook. He retched at the thought of that. Beautiful Nat savaged by the rocks, by the hooks of fishermen and the fish that were out there. Would any of her face be recognisable now? He had images of her being pulled out limb by limb, scraping blood and bone of the rocks. He gagged, trying to keep the contents of his stomach inside. After a while he gave up, what was the point?

## CHAPTER 31 – WAITING TIME

It was two days of waiting. Two days of trying to keep down the food they gave him, and his mind each time thought back to Nat's mauled body. He could not keep it down, and didn't want to. There were voices around him, there always were but he had not heard a word they said. His one job was to get them to find Nat, and find the tramp. Whatever they needed, he would assist them. Being in a cell was now not new to him, but he didn't pace like before. There was no restless energy. His body had given up, his brain too. Now was the time to wait for the inevitable.

The policeman had taken him to the interview every now and then to question him, breaking him out of his trance. He had many more questions than Ash had thought; "How did you meet Nat?", "Did you kill Jack Hawkins?", "Did you plan this altogether?", "Are you lying for anyone?". They had not found the tramp, had not found Nat and were starting to become suspicious of his story. "In my knowledge, it is very rare to get someone walk in to the police station and confess to a crime. It is even more unlikely for their confession to be true. Who are you covering for? Did your uncle put you up to this? Do you need protection? Because we can provide that. At the moment we are wasting a lot of police resources, on what could be a made up story. How can you prove that a man killed Nat? How can you prove that she is dead?"

All Ash said was, "Look for her. Find her, let her have some peace. I'm only here for her, I wish to god it didn't happen but it did."

As Ash stewed in the cell, there were only his thoughts for company. He had turned up at the police station, to confess. It was the ultimate act of contrition to be open and honest about all of his failings. And he had told his story but it did not seem like they believed him. According to the officer, most confessions are either immediately when a crime has been committed, after long hours of interrogation or if somebody wants to protect somebody they knew committed a crime. They had asked him why had he not just phoned 999 when she had gone in? Instead he had waited a few hours and then gone to the police station. He did not have an answer for that. It had not occurred to Ash at any point that the police would have any knowledge of Ash's activities over the last few months. As it turns out, they did.

They were very keen to ask questions about Chris and Matt. What were there jobs? Why was Ash staying with his uncle for so long? Did Ash ever do any work for them? He knew when to keep his mouth shut. The grim image of glee on Vinny's face when he was cleaning his knives was all Ash needed to keep his lips tightly sealed. In one of the many interrogations, Ash asked the officer why he was not being taken seriously. He had then been offered a deal, if Ash told all he knew about Chris, they would look for Nat. There was no more conversation after that.

It did occur to Ash afterwards, they obviously had to investigate his claims about what happened, and would be in a lot of trouble if her body came floating up after they had ignored a clear cut confession. He had had a permanent dry retch in his throat the whole time he had been at the station. When the time came, it was not the dour policeman that gave him the news but the custody sergeant. "You are one lucky man. Free release, and no charges. One very lucky man indeed. Not even a wasting police time charge. You best get out of here quick."

## CHAPTER 32 – RETRIBUTION

Out into the light stepped a rather shell shocked Ash. It had taken a good thirty minutes for him to leave the cell, at one point they had threatened to lock him back up. He would have taken the offer. No one would give him the time of day, or an answer. Onwards the police station bustled, and forgot about Ash. He had been ready to give it all up, he had given it all up. Yet they hadn't thrown away the key. Most of his nausea had gone now, he still felt sick however it was not a permanent pain in his throat. Despondently now, he had stepped out onto the street. It was not clear why they had let him go, maybe his uncle had done something to sort it all out. He couldn't imagine what would have possibly erased a whole crime with evidence, or was sure he did not want to know.

All sorts of possibilities were going through his head: Should he look for the body? Should he find the tramp? What about going to the newspapers? Surely they would lap this up. Police not arresting murderer and accomplice? It would be a Daily Mail showcase for weeks.

And then he saw her. There was no mistaking that red hair, or way she held herself. He had stopped short when he saw her, and the crowd of people walking past him tutted as they moved around him. People could have been firing guns down the street and he would not have moved. Nat walked up to him, heels clicking as she strode towards him. Her hand snaked out and slapped him hard. It barely registered to him, and even if he had seen it coming, he would not have done anything.

"H...How?" he whispered.

"How? How you fucker? Well when I realised no one was coming to save me I swam to shore. I thought you might have been too much of a pussy to swim but surely you could have thrown a fucking rubber ring off the side?"

There were scratches up her arm, and her eye was purple. She was glaring at him. And she had a right to. Ash realised that if she wanted to drag him into the sea and drown him, that he didn't really disagree with her.

"I..I didn't think it would go that far?"

"Go that far? You fucking set me up, try to trap me and then bundle me off into the fucking ocean? Did you think we were going to kiss and make up? You sicken me." She slapped him again, he did not react.

Tears were in his eyes again, they had not really stopped over the last few days.

"That was never the plan, I thought you were a murderer. We were going to take you in."

"Well that worked didn't it? How does one go from being a sanctimonious poundshop Sherlock Holmes to offing someone? Did you just slip and decide to smash my face into a wall?"
"That was not me, and you know it. I was just there to find out what happened. About... well Dean and Jack."

"So you just randomly had a guy set up to off me just in case?"
"It was his idea."

"Well who the fuck was he? One of your uncle's henchmen?"
"No, you know him. It was Dean's dad."

"Oh shit."

"Yeah oh shit."

Nat stopped short at that. She seemed to hesitate for a second before she spoke. She choked a little as she said, "You know what really hurts? I thought I was through with this. I had a clean start. I even met someone who wasn't more than half shit. You betrayed me and you did it.. You did it because you think I'm a monster. That I am so horrid that I should be eradicated."

"That's not true."

"Well it sure looks like it from here. At the very least you were convinced I was a murderer. You chose to believe the worst in me, that I was capable of not only killing people, but that I vindictively, coldly, set out to destroy those who wronged me. At the worst you were actively conspiring to kill me. Well actually, no, you would have just fucking killed me if the tide was out. You are scum."

Holding her head in her hands, she stopped her tirade. Ash motioned her to a bench and she raised her hand when he stepped to her. He moved back as fast as he could, hands help up in a surrender pose and then pointed to a nearby bench. When she sat down, he sat on the cold floor a few feet away.

"I couldn't live with it. I don't know whether they told you, but I walked to the police station and handed myself in. I told them everything."

Nat laughed at that, a short sound with no humour in it, "Naïve, saint Ash. Why the fuck would I care? You still did it. You could walk out in front of traffic now and I wouldn't even blink. You're dead to me."

"I don't believe that," Ash said. Nat looked up sharply at that. "No?" She replied, daring him to go on.

"No. I deserve all the abuse I get. A lifetime of it, for sure. But if you wanted me dead and buried, or to suffer even more. You know what you had to do?"

"No?" She replied again.

"Not fucking turn up. Go disappear for a few years, I would have been convicted. Or while I was rotting in that jail cell confessing every sin I have ever even thought, you know what you could have done? Said yeah you see that fucker, he just tried to kill me. Attempted murder is not much different than murder in the grand scheme of things. And however much I did not want it to happen, I was a part of it."

The silence stretched as she looked off into the distance. Her knees now tucked under her chin in a protective pose. Ash wanted to help, but he had already caused enough damage.

"Let's be honest, there's still time for that. I have ruined absolutely everything. Whatever you want from me, you can have it. You want me to walk straight back into that station? I will do it. I mean shit, it took me long enough to leave when they told me. Now you're here we could go together. Would that be enough?"

"You're serious aren't you?" She asked.

"Yes, yes I am," and he realised he was. The sense of nausea had definitely dissipated, but the lurch in his stomach was still there. He felt like he'd just taken a dive off a cliff, and he hadn't landed yet. "I will do whatever you want, I can't make it right. But how can I try?" It took a long time for Nat to respond, Ash was still stuck in his pose, arms pointed to the station.

"I don't know. I am goddamn angry with you, murderously so. I would like to see you suffer, and I have thought about drowning you. I have thought a lot of nasty thoughts, and I think it's fair to say I am not being unreasonable. I just want to know why? Why does this happen to me? All the people in the world and I find Dean. He then dies, then I found you and this shitstorm or whatever it is. How the fuck does this happen?"

"I.. I don't know about Dean, and I can't speak for him. Me? Well I thought you killed a man. I think you are wonderful, beautiful and amazing. I thought you were capable of killing someone, and you had the opportunity to do it. With somebody telling me about Dean, well I believed it all. Gullible, naïve Ash right?" Nat was sobbing silently, "Fuck you, you don't get to judge, Mr holier than thou. How do you get to be the judge of what is right?" "I don't. I was wrong in the worst way. But you wanted to know. Why did I do it? I simply believed you could. Now, I'm not going to recover from this."

"You? You are not going to recover from this?" She raged. "No, No I'm not. Whatever you do, I will know that I can't come back from this. How could I? I'm a dead man pretending to be alive."

"I'm done." Nat stood up " I'm done with this town, with shitty men and with you. I'm going to walk away. I'm not coming back. If I ever see you again, I can't be held responsible for my actions. I don't know how we got here, but it's over," she went to leave and turned to him, "I hope it burns you up, and eats you inside. We could have been wonderful, you could have had a life. I never betrayed you, I only helped. I never gave up on you. You've torn what pathetic piece of existence you had into tiny pieces, and taken mine with it. I hope you suffer every day of your life, and at the end of that miserable torment, that lifetime would be a drop in the ocean to what you have done to me."

And with that she walked, heels clicking in the distance as she disappeared.

Ash retched there and then. Crawling he hauled himself up onto the bench, and put his head in his hands. This was rock bottom. There was not a way out, and he wasn't looking for one anymore. He had set out into the big wide world, and it turned out it was shit. Tears rolled down his face, and passers-by gave him a wide birth as he fell into his despair. Never before had it occurred to him, that he was a bad person. Everyone was capable of bad things, but he had never thought of himself as... well.. as a bad guy. Murder was not something that was in his capabilities, and yet here he was. He had lied, trafficked drugs and to top it all off was an accessory to attempted murder. He had acted with good intentions, and fell from one fuck up to the next. It was simple in the end, Nat was a good person. An actual human being, capable of love and life. Ash was scum. No other outcomes were plausible, or in fact true. He had some decisions to make, about life and what to do next and he would make them. Not for now though, he would simply sit until he couldn't anymore. He would remember a time where he had a hope for the future.

Hours or seconds later, something made him look up. Everyone had been walking around him for hours, and the traffic had gently slowed as day turned to night. Ash looked up in time to see Vinny standing over him, hooded in the rain. "You should have kept your mouth shut," he said. Something silver flashed as he stepped close to Ash. Vinny walked away, Ash let out a gasp as blood poured from his torso. He slid down the bench, hands clasped to his side half-heartedly. He let out a short laugh as he laid back, the rain gently falling down. He didn't bother to ask for help, just laid back thinking: It's just a drop in the ocean.

# THE END

## ABOUT THE AUTHOR

If you got this far, well done you. I would love a share, a message or a review. Feel free to heckle as much as you want.

I plan to write many books, and they will be bigger and better as they go. This was my first and of course I have made mistakes, thank you for reading despite them.

This book took forever to write. I truly never thought I would get this far.

Now I can officially say I am an author.


Instagram account: @roastmybook

Printed in Great Britain
by Amazon